THE COST OF *Eternity*

SHAYLA KERSTEN

ELLORA'S CAVE
ROMANTICA PUBLISHING

What the critics are saying...

&

"Ms. Kersten has once again created a story that is compelling for the reader. The Cost of Eternity is a mixture of erotic scenes with suspense and drama that ensnares the reader until the final word." ~ *Fallen Angels Review*

An Ellora's Cave Romantica Publication

www.ellorascave.com

The Cost of Eternity

ISBN 9781419956652
ALL RIGHTS RESERVED.
The Cost of Eternity Copyright © 2007 Shayla Kersten
Edited by Mary Moran
Photography and cover art by Les Byerley

Electronic book Publication February 2007
Trade paperback Publication June 2007

This book has been printed in the U.S.A. by Jasmine-Jade Enterprises, LLC.

Excerpt from *Burning Hunger* Copyright © Tawny Taylor, 2007

With the exception of quotes used in reviews, this book may not be reproduced or used in whole or in part by any means existing without written permission from the publisher, Ellora's Cave Publishing, Inc.® 1056 Home Avenue, Akron OH 44310-3502.

This book is a work of fiction and any resemblance to persons, living or dead, or places, events or locales is purely coincidental. The characters are productions of the authors' imagination and used fictitiously.

Content Advisory:

S – ENSUOUS
E – ROTIC
X – TREME

Ellora's Cave Publishing offers three levels of Romantica™ reading entertainment: S (S-ensuous), E (E-rotic), and X (X-treme).

The following material contains graphic sexual content meant for mature readers. This story has been rated E–rotic.

S-*ensuous* love scenes are explicit and leave nothing to the imagination.

E-*rotic* love scenes are explicit, leave nothing to the imagination, and are high in volume per the overall word count. E-rated titles might contain material that some readers find objectionable—in other words, almost anything goes, sexually. E-rated titles are the most graphic titles we carry in terms of both sexual language and descriptiveness in these works of literature.

X-*treme* titles differ from E-rated titles only in plot premise and storyline execution. Stories designated with the letter X tend to contain difficult or controversial subject matter not for the faint of heart.

About the Author

By day, Shayla Kersten is a mild-mannered accountant. By night, she's a writer of sexy romances. Torn between genres, Shayla writes erotic stories about hot heroes and their sexy women as well as hot men and their passionate heroes.

A native of Arkansas, Shayla spent four years in the Army as a missile specialist, stationed in Germany and Oklahoma. After her enlistment was up, she spent eleven years in New York City taking a bite out of the Big Apple. Even her love of theatre and the nightlife of the big city couldn't cure terminal homesickness for the Natural State. In 1995 she returned to her roots in Arkansas.

Shayla now divides her time between her mother, her spoiled-rotten dogs, her dratted day job and her obsession — writing. And no, her mother doesn't know what she writes. That's between Shayla, her dogs and her readers!

Shayla welcomes comments from readers. You can find her website and email address on her author bio page at www.ellorascave.com.

Tell Us What You Think
We appreciate hearing reader opinions about our books. You can email us at Comments@EllorasCave.com.

THE COST OF ETERNITY
ಬ

Acknowledgements

❧

To Myla Jackson and Delilah Devlin for encouragement and guiding me down the path toward publication.

To Layla Chase for her patience.

To the Mt. Helicon Muses for more than I can possibly fit here.

To the women of Kharities.

Trademarks Acknowledgement

❧

The author acknowledges the trademarked status and trademark owners of the following wordmarks mentioned in this work of fiction:

- Lexus: Toyota Jidosha Kabushiki Kaisha, t/a Toyota Motor Corporation
- New York University: New York University Corporation
- Tylenol: Tylenol Company, The Corporation New Jersey

Chapter One

The young Asian woman stood silent, watching him. With a practiced eye, Lorcan MacKenna's gaze traveled up and down her slight frame. The formfitting silk dress hid nothing. Buttons ranged from the high collar around her delectable neck to the hem just above the knee. The bright red color matched her pouting lips. Her slim almost boyish figure was most appealing. Maybe too appealing.

He brushed aside thoughts of a more masculine partner. Men, while more to his liking, were too dangerous, too easy to become involved with. Female prostitutes left him satisfied physically without the danger of emotional ties.

"Strip."

Her hands moved languidly to the first button. With a deliberate slowness she parted the material, revealing small pert breasts half covered with lace from the low-cut bra. As the dress slid to the ground, the soft rustle of silk whispered. Her lips curved into a knowing smile. She reached for the clasp of her bra.

"Stop," he ordered. "Leave it." Her dark brown areolas and tiny nipples peeking through the lace made his cock twitch. A garter belt held up her stockings, showing off her bare crotch. A tiny triangle of tight black curls dotted the top of her slit.

She slipped her fingers in the waist of the garter.

"Leave those as well," he said. Lorcan hadn't moved from the large, comfortable wingback chair. His silk brocade dressing gown was cool against his swelling erection. His gaze raked over her body again.

"Suck me." His voice was no more than a rough whisper. This is what she was here for and her efforts were well paid.

Without hesitation, she walked toward him.

Lorcan moved his legs apart, allowing her to kneel between them. He shivered as her small hands reached for the edges of his robe.

Parting the silk with unhurried care, she reached down to grasp his shaft. It filled and lengthened, her small hand unable to wrap around the girth.

"Suck it," he growled at her hesitation.

She dipped her head to his cock and licked the tip before her lips encircled the head and she took him in her mouth.

The slight sting of teeth grazed his sensitive flesh. "Yes…" Lorcan's breath sighed.

She swallowed him deeper. Her tongue moved against the sensitive underside of his shaft. In long, slow strokes, her mouth slid up and down his flesh. Both hands wrapped around the base, stroking him in rhythm with her mouth.

His hips began to rock, matching her movements. The blood-red lipstick smeared on his cock fascinated him.

She licked her way around the head, sucking the sensitive area below the crown. The hot mouth never stopped.

Leaning back, he let the sounds of her work wash over him. Wet sucking noises, soft gasps for air, skin rubbing against his hot, hard flesh. His keen hearing reveled in the sounds as much as his body enjoyed her movements. As the scent of her arousal wafted up, his hands clenched the armrests of the chair. The rapid pulse under her heated skin gave off an even more appealing scent. Her soft moan vibrated through the intimate contact of her mouth.

One of her hands moved away. The sound of her fingers working her wet hole and the smell of her pungent arousal excited him.

His hips undulated slowly, fucking her mouth as her fingers thrust into her pussy. "Oh yes," he whispered. His balls tightened, preparing for the finale, but he didn't want to finish in her mouth. Lorcan's eyes flew open then he grabbed the woman between his legs. A surprised moan escaped her mouth as he lifted her head from his erection. He stood, slung her around and pushed her onto the chair on her knees.

Her hands clenched the back of the chair. The scratching of her nails digging into the upholstery added fuel to the fire in his body.

Lorcan knew his fingers would leave bruises as he pulled her ass toward him. His aching cock invaded her tight, wet pussy with roughness brought on by sharp need. He wrapped his arms around her slight body and thrust hard.

Her cries of pleasure mingled with whimpers of pain.

"Yes," Lorcan moaned as his seed rushed to the surface. With hard strokes, he massaged her slick clit. He needed her to come. Only her release could give him what he needed.

Thrusting violently, her body tensed as she screamed her orgasm.

Heat scalded his dick as he erupted in her body. His lips curled back from the razor-sharp fangs that penetrated her neck. The rush of orgasm paled in comparison to the heat of the crimson liquid flowing from her neck.

She shivered with shock as he drank deep, her endorphin-laced blood rushing through his veins. Her feverish body began to chill, warning him to stop.

With regret his mouth released its hold. His tongue snaked out to catch the cooling drops forming near the tiny wounds.

She went limp in his arms. Her body still pressed close, the weak but steady pulse of her heart reassured him.

With one last remorseful lick at the fang marks, he lifted her unconscious body in his arms. A few strides across the room brought him to the wide bed, the covers already pulled back. He deposited her gently then covered her with the tenderness of a lover.

She was so small Lorcan couldn't take much from her, but what he received was excellent. He didn't even know her name, didn't want to. The agency he used knew it. He forbade the women to introduce themselves, ask his name or even speak. Picked up by his chauffeur and delivered to his apartment, they were returned the next day in the same manner. Many years had passed since he had taken a life but this one tempted him. To be able to drink all of the amazing elixir from her veins...

Other vampires fed on fear, but Lorcan was addicted to the endorphins of sex.

Lorcan sighed as he brushed dark hair from her forehead. Almost a hundred years had passed since his last lover and he missed the companionship and comfort. However the pain of losing them made him vow never to let his emotions become involved again. He left the room without looking back, knowing this situation was as good as it would get.

* * * * *

Lorcan found Tomas waiting patiently outside the room. As he strode past, he nodded. Tomas would make sure the woman was all right and send her on her way in the morning. He had been with Lorcan for many years, more years than Lorcan cared to think.

When Lorcan first chose him, Tomas O'Dwyer had been a young man. Now his silver hair was receding and deep wrinkles lined his somber face.

Soon Lorcan would need to choose a new body servant. He thought of Tomas as more than a servant. He was a trusted friend and in a weird sort of way, a kinsman.

Tomas descended from Lorcan's sister Catriona. The youngest of his eight siblings, she died in 1813. Lorcan kept tabs on his family's progeny and always picked servants from within the circle. Several kinsmen worked for him at his various homes and hideouts in different countries. The family still whispered about the "curse" placed on Lorcan MacKenna in 1798 but only those close to him knew the truth.

His robe rustled around him as he wandered down the dark hallway. Lorcan had been in the New York apartment for almost ten years now. Originally purchased in 1848, the apartment had been completely rebuilt after a fire nearly fifty years ago. The high-vaulted ceilings and dark paneling were old-fashioned but the décor suited him. Maybe it had something to do with being over two hundred years old.

When people questioned his eternal thirty-something age, he moved. In an earlier era, hiding his immortality was easier. Borders didn't require proof of identity, people didn't question the lord of the manor and if a person disappeared, well, there weren't forensic specialists to figure out how they died.

The move into the twenty-first century was difficult on a creature who fed on the blood of others. Apart from a few trusted servants, he was isolated in a suddenly much smaller world and the loneliness was complete.

Sometimes he wondered if eternal life was worth being alone forever. Friends and servants—lovers when he dared have them—all aged and died, leaving him alone. He grieved for them and continued to face the endless night. After his last lover's death, almost a hundred years ago, Lorcan had considered ending the solitude. However his sense of self-preservation was too strong. Everything about him pushed him to live. He long ago decided the predatory nature of his kind refused to let him end his life. To hunt and to win was part of their basic design. Senses, hearing, sight, smell—all heightened by the change ensured their survival.

The heavy oak door of his bedroom beckoned. Closing the door behind him, Lorcan let the robe slide from his body. His veins still rushed with the thrill of fresh blood. Crawling onto the massive bed, he let the memory flow over him. Plans to ask for the young woman again formed in his mind. A woman so aroused by giving a blowjob was a rare find. Normally more time was spent before bringing a woman to the point he wanted before feeding.

His cock twitched with the fresh infusion of blood. Lorcan gently stroked the hardening flesh, wishing he dared return to the woman, dared take more from her nubile body. He sighed as a sense of weakness filled him. Although shuttered against the day in his room, he knew when the sun began its travels across the sky. He let the rising sun usher him into dreamless slumber, his hand still caressing his half-hard erection.

Chapter Two

ಐ

The November night was cool and damp, chilling Lorcan to the bone. As he wandered the darkness, he pulled his long coat tighter against the elements. The moon sank toward the horizon in the hours before the dawn. As the sun prepared to wipe away the night his pulse quickened with a sense of urgency. While checking his territory, he had wandered the streets of New York for hours. The city had been his almost since his creator brought him over.

Vampires were protective of their domain. Only one dared set up residence in a given city. Unfortunately for this very reason, he could never permanently banish the loneliness. The memory of his last love washed over him like the cold night air. A vision of Gustave's laughing dark eyes brought back the pain he wanted to avoid.

When Lorcan realized the depth of their feelings, he believed their relationship would survive the change. After a hundred years, Lorcan could still taste the sweetness of his lover's blood as he drank deeply, taking him to the edge of death. The weak caress of Gustave's lips sucking Lorcan's open vein made him rub the memory of the wound on his wrist.

But their relationship hadn't lasted. Within weeks, Gustave became restless and increasingly irritable. Lorcan realized his mistake too late. Blinded by his feelings to what was happening, Lorcan hadn't taken precautions for Gustave's life without him. Money, a safe place for his lover to live, would have ensured his safety. Gustave left one night without a word of goodbye. When Lorcan finally found his trail, it was too late.

Lorcan should have known Gustave would return home to his native Paris. Marius, the resident vampire, had no tolerance for trespassers. He had gotten there first and Gustave was dead. All Lorcan had done by bringing him across was accelerate their permanent separation.

Marius' mocking words taunted him into a rage and in the end, the dark Romanian vampire lay headless on the cobblestones of his Paris home. Lorcan still claimed the property there but couldn't bring himself to visit it.

The sounds of a scuffle pulled him from his sorrow-filled memories. A dark alley, a dark sound and the smell of arousal assaulted his senses. Turning to peer into the darkness, his unnatural night vision showed the shadowy figures of four men surrounding someone kneeling on the ground. He slipped into the shadows. As he drew closer, he could see two of the men had their cocks hanging out of opened jeans. Lorcan knew he shouldn't interfere but the sounds and the smells, especially the pungent smell of male arousal, drew him deeper into the alley.

One of the men yanked at the blond shoulder-length hair of their victim—a young man.

"You said you'd blow me for twenty bucks, so blow me," the man growled. Tall and heavily muscled, the man's rough treatment inspired terror on the young man's face. The shadow of a tattoo on the side of the man's bull neck caught Lorcan's attention for a moment. Fingers twisted in the blond hair as the man pulled his victim's face against his erection. "Suck it!"

Lorcan could almost taste the acrid fear rising off the blond man as he opened his mouth to comply. Lorcan's own arousal hardened at the sight of the young man's attempt to swallow the dick. The tattooed man gave up waiting and pulled hard at the long strands with both hands. Holding his victim's head still, he thrust, fucking the man's mouth.

The glistening of tears marked the young man's face as he took the abuse.

A tight band of sympathy gripped Lorcan's heart and batted back the rush of arousal.

"I don't want to wait." A second man, the white of a scar bisecting his cheek, moved behind the victim, grabbing the waist of his tattered jeans. As he hauled him to his feet, the young man moaned in pain as the first man maintained his grip on the long hair. Scarface reached around to fumble with the struggling victim's fly.

The other two men, waiting their turn, grabbed his arms to help hold their prey still.

The young man struggled violently, his hands pushing at the hips of the tattooed man. Fear overcame the obvious pain of the fingers twisting into his hair. Pulling free of the cock in his mouth, the young man moaned in fear and pain. "No!" he yelled. "I don't do that!"

The tattooed man released his hair long enough to hit him hard across the face.

A dark smear appeared on the young man's mouth.

The exhilarating aroma of blood mixed with the earthy scent of arousal caused Lorcan to stifle a gasp.

Tattoo spoke with a threatening growl. "You'll do what we want. And if we're not satisfied, you won't get paid."

The smirk left no doubt in Lorcan's mind the promised money would never change hands.

The dick forced back into his mouth muffled the young man's protests.

Lorcan couldn't stand silent any longer. It was one thing to watch a hooker trading his wares in an alley, another to watch a gang rape. In complete silence, he moved closer in the shadows. Finally within a few feet of the five men, he stepped into the pale yellow illumination of a distant streetlight.

"What have we here?" Lorcan asked, his voice a low growl.

The four would-be rapists looked at him, their gazes darted between each other and Lorcan.

Their victim looked as if he weren't sure whether to be relieved or afraid of another person joining his attackers.

Scarface regained his composure first and snarled, "Are you looking for trouble? Or you wanna take his place?"

"If there's trouble, you're the ones who have found it." Lorcan rolled back and forth slightly on the balls of his feet, hands at his sides with fingers loose. Experience told him the nonchalant confidence would make them think twice. "The young man has a previous engagement and won't be able to play any more tonight."

Mouths open in surprise, the four men looked at each other quickly. Their thoughts were too easy to read. There were four in their group and, even if the young man joined him, Lorcan would be outnumbered four to two. Their lust obscured the dark brooding threat in Lorcan's soft baritone.

Lorcan wasn't a big man. At a lean, wiry five-eleven, he could easily be mistaken as a non-threat. They couldn't be more wrong. Even without the inhuman strength of a vampire, Lorcan had hundreds of years of training to back up his words.

"I think you gentlemen should run along and find another playmate. Doing so would be easier all around and definitely less painful on your part." The hidden sheaths in Lorcan's gums itched. His territorial nature brought out the urge to dispose of this trash. They might not realize they were trespassing, but it didn't lessen their danger for the transgression.

Something in his voice or his stance must have sparked comprehension. The man holding the victim's hair eased his fingers out of the tangled mess.

Lorcan smelled fear as Tattoo tucked his now-wilted dick back in his jeans.

"Come on, guys," Tattoo said, his voice rough with false bravado. "It's not worth it. This piece of shit can't suck cock to save his life."

The other men inched away, toward the other end of the alley, when Tattoo pulled something from his back pocket. Lorcan moved quickly but not fast enough to prevent a small billy club from making contact with the young man's head. The copper smell of fresh blood caught his attention as the four men ran from the alley.

"Damn," Lorcan muttered. He leaned over to check the young man's pulse. Steady if fast. "What do I do with him now?" He planned to see the young man away from his would-be rapists and leave him to his own devices. Now Lorcan couldn't walk away. If the wound didn't kill the pale blond man, someone might find him here and finish the job.

Why didn't Lorcan learn to mind his own business?

* * * * *

Lorcan stood nearby and watched Tomas clean the young man's injury with a gentle touch. He hadn't regained consciousness. Getting him back to the apartment had proved difficult. Even in the early hours before dawn lugging an unconscious man through the streets of New York could be dangerous. Lorcan scrubbed his face with the palm of his hand. "Well?"

"A few stitches would be a good idea but I'm not equipped to do it. Should I call a doctor?"

"Did he have any ID? Anyone we could contact?"

"Nothing except some change and a key in his pockets."

Lorcan sighed. Pawning the young man off on someone who knew him was an easier solution. "Do you know a doctor you can trust?" Lorcan finally asked.

Tomas straightened from his task. "Yes."

"Do it," Lorcan said abruptly. He dropped into the wingback chair near the fireplace as Tomas gathered his first-aid supplies. The sun had risen nearly an hour ago. Its presence was sapping his strength and the effort of getting the young man to the apartment hadn't helped. Almost a week had passed since the Asian woman had serviced Lorcan's needs. He needed blood.

Lorcan's gaze rested on the young man. The dark blond hair spread out against the pillow. He and Tomas had stripped him of the clothes he wore before putting him into the bed. A muscled frame hid beneath the well-worn clothes. He was thin but still managed to maintain his muscle tone. His waist was narrow as were his hips. An unruly patch of blondish hair surrounded his flaccid circumcised cock. Lorcan shivered with desire at the memory. The blankets now obscured the object of his thoughts but he wondered what it would look like hard and aching.

Lorcan stood abruptly, shaking the idea from his mind. Almost a hundred years had passed since he had taken a man sexually. Not since Gustave. He had, when the need arose, fed on men, but he relied on the adrenaline of terror to infuse the blood with a more satisfying jolt. The hard planes of a man's body against his would make the memory of losing Gustave too painful.

Lorcan paced around the room on silent feet. His thoughts, the young man, the lack of blood, made him jittery. He needed to rest but he hesitated leaving the stranger unattended. A soft moan caught his attention and he was by the bed in two swift strides.

"You're safe." Lorcan's voice was a soft whisper.

The young man's deep blue eyes were open and wide with fear.

"You're safe here." Lorcan spoke a little louder.

Lorcan was already falling into the depths of those eyes. Now *he* was the one in danger. His hand moved of its own volition, caressing the stubble-roughened face. A shiver of desire rushed through him. "What's your name?"

The man swallowed hard.

Lorcan imagined not many people asked or even cared what his name was as long as his mouth was available.

"Kevin," he whispered. "Kevin St. James."

"Well, Kevin, there's a doctor on the way. You need a few stitches and then you'll be good as new."

Lorcan didn't think Kevin could become any paler but he did.

His hands flew to his face, terror in his eyes. "My face?"

Lorcan shook his head. "Here." He reached to touch the side of his head. Evidently, Kevin was a vain young man. "No one will ever know."

Relief filled the big blue eyes.

"I have a chance at an audition. They'd never take me with a scar..." Kevin's voice cut off, choked by a stifled sob. "I shouldn't have... But I needed the money..." His hands clutched at the blankets. "What have I done?" The hands started shaking first then his body followed as shock set in.

Compassion rose in his chest and Lorcan couldn't stop himself. He sat on the bed and gathered the frightened man in his arms. Savoring the warm body against his own, he murmured soft nonsense in his ear. Kevin's arms, hesitant at first, circled Lorcan, tightening as tears finally escaped and the sobs deepened. The strong grip of a man's arms around him caused Lorcan's cock to stir with desire. As he comforted the distraught man, he pushed aside the feeling. He was startled out of his thoughts when the door opened behind him.

"Sir, the doctor will be here soon."

"Thank you, Tomas." His words were automatic. The man in his arms distracted his mind and body. The door closed with a soft snick. Lorcan held the trembling man until sleep reclaimed him and for a long time afterward.

* * * * *

After the doctor left, Lorcan watched Kevin sleep for a few minutes then left the room with silent regret. Exhaustion wrapped around him like a fog. He needed rest. Even more, he needed to feed but it had to wait. Rest would have to do for now.

Once in his room, he stripped with slow, stumbling movements as he shuffled toward the bed. Lorcan reeled from more than hunger as he sprawled across the soft sheets. Desire for the despairing young man coursed through him. His cock roused even as his body protested with fatigue. The thought of Kevin kneeling at his feet, his full lips circling the crown of his dick, made Lorcan ache. His fingers mimicked his fantasy, wrapping around the head, tightening like the lips of a lover.

His mind envisioned a soft tongue licking slowly, laving the slit, sucking the moisture. He could almost feel the hot mouth traveling the length, licking, nibbling, only to return to suckle the tip again. As he stroked his heated flesh, his mind's eye watched Kevin's mouth engulf him deep. Lorcan's free hand moved down to fondle his balls. He pictured Kevin's hand there, teasing, rolling them gently. His fantasy so real, he arched his hips into his hand as he imagined pushing deeper into Kevin's mouth.

Lorcan's balls tightened as his thoughts turned from Kevin's mouth to his ass. The thought of pushing his cock into the younger man's tight, hot hole was too much. Come shot from his dick, streams of hot, white liquid landing on his stomach and chest.

"Oh shit," he mumbled. Gasping for air, he barely finished milking his cock before exhaustion, combined with the afterglow of his orgasm, overtook him.

Chapter Three
೧೨

Warmth and safety suffused Kevin as he woke. He couldn't remember the last time he'd awoken feeling so protected. In the neighborhood where he lived, his apartment didn't inspire a feeling of safety. The scent of fresh, clean bedding filled his nostrils before the smell of his own body overwhelmed him. The acrid odor of sweat permeated his skin. The dingy furnished apartment he called home had a permanent stench but it was a roof over his head and the rent was reasonable.

But he needed extra cash and fast. So he followed the really screwed-up advice of a fellow actor. Well, not really. The suggestion was an escort agency. Kevin was too afraid of someone finding out. Too many stories of well-known actors with their skeletons falling out of their closets. Not to mention his own family... His way seemed to guarantee anonymity.

The first night, he managed to service two men before his stomach churned with disgust. Those men hadn't wanted anyone to see them. They finished quickly and left him in the stinking alley where they'd used him.

The second night—last night—Kevin hadn't seen the other three men following him and the tattooed man into the alley. Once he had, he had been so sure he wouldn't leave there alive. When the dark man appeared, he thought he was dreaming. Then the pain and darkness. Waking up to find the man again, find himself wrapped in strong, comforting arms and safe...

His throat caught as he thought about what almost happened. They would have raped him, maybe killed him. In his mind, he thanked the dark angel who had saved him.

The sound of the door opening filled him with hope of seeing his rescuer. Instead, the tall, silver-haired man called Tomas entered the room.

"You're awake. Good," he said as he deposited a tray on the table near the fireplace. "Here's something to eat. The bathroom is through there."

He pointed toward a closed door Kevin hadn't noticed.

"I would recommend a shower. Soon." The man's smile softened the implication. "There's also some Tylenol on the tray if your head hurts. Call if you need anything." Tomas took a thick robe from the closet and tossed it on the foot of the bed.

"Th-thank you," Kevin stammered. The kindness of these people confounded him. And a shower sounded even better than the food smelled.

"You're welcome," Tomas replied as he left the room.

* * * * *

The stream of hot water felt so good on his aching muscles, Kevin must have stood under the showerhead for almost an hour. The hot water in his apartment never lasted very long.

Wiping the steamy mirror, Kevin stared at his reflection. He was thin, too thin. To save money he'd been eating only when he worked at the restaurant. Staff were allowed a free meal each shift. Between less food and stress over a big audition being just out of his reach, he'd dropped a few pounds.

Maybe he should have called his mother and asked for the money. But then his stepfather probably wouldn't let her send it. His big-shot stepfather made it very clear he wouldn't help him. Walter was afraid Kevin's career choices would cause him to look bad, somehow soil his political career. Having a no-good actor wannabe as a stepson didn't look good in his Washington circles.

He shook off the funk threatening to engulf him. A meal awaited him and his stomach reminded him of its neglect. A toothbrush, still in the package, was on the bathroom counter as was a razor. Although he made quick use of the toothbrush, Kevin was too hungry to take the time to shave. Not eating worried him more for his job prospects than for the hunger itself. He needed to maintain muscle mass. Starving was a quick way to lose his tone.

When Kevin came out of the bathroom, the bedroom was still dark. Only a small lamp on the table by the tray and the fire lit the room. He had no idea what time it was. Pushing aside the curtain, Kevin found shutters on the windows, blocking any light from getting through. He looked around for a clock but found none. His stomach snarled at his curiosity.

His gaze focused on the tray of food. Pulling the cover off the dish, he had a forkful of grilled potatoes headed for his mouth before his ass hit the chair. The roast was tender enough to cut with a fork, which was good, since in his impatience, he probably wouldn't have bothered with a knife. Even though the food had cooled during his shower, Kevin thought it was the best thing he had ever tasted.

He made quick work of the food, probably too quick. His stomach wasn't accustomed to so much and ached slightly with his overindulgence. Sitting in the quiet room and staring at the fire caused his eyes to droop with sleep. He should find his clothes and leave but he couldn't force his languid limbs to function. For the first time in months he felt relaxed, comfortable. He should be worried about being at the mercy of the dark-haired stranger. The school of hard knocks should have taught him to be less trusting, but he couldn't find it in himself to be suspicious of his benefactor.

The memory of the man's arms around him, the soft crooned words of comfort, made apprehension impossible. A shiver of desire coursed through him. Even though he'd wondered about men, about being with a man, Kevin had always suppressed the thoughts deep in the darkest reaches of his mind. The men he'd serviced did nothing for him, in spite of the hidden desires. But the dark-haired man... The thought of tasting his cock, letting him fuck his mouth, caused Kevin's dick to twitch in spite of his extreme fatigue.

His dark angel wasn't strikingly handsome like some of the actors Kevin knew. His dark, almost black hair was a mass of unruly curls. A slightly olive complexion gave him an exotic look. Something about his dark green eyes made him attractive in a way Kevin couldn't fully describe. And whatever it was, Kevin wanted him close, wanted the strong arms around him. Brushing away the thought, he decided gratitude made him feel this way.

Kevin knew if he didn't get up, he'd fall asleep in the chair. From the corner, the bed beckoned. Shaking with weakness, he stood then stumbled across to the bed. Without thinking, he shed the warm robe and crawled under the covers.

*****

"He's sleeping again," Tomas said as he encountered Lorcan in the hallway.

Lorcan followed the older man's gaze as Tomas eyed his robe. Impatient to check on Kevin, he had risen quickly and hadn't bothered to dress. "Did he eat?"

Tomas lifted the cover from the empty plate. "Quite well. I'm surprised he was able to finish it. He looks as if he hasn't eaten much lately."

Lorcan nodded. His gaze moved from the empty plate to linger on the door to Kevin's room.

"I doubt he would hear you if you checked on him," Tomas said, continuing toward the kitchen.

Lorcan smiled at his retreating back. Tomas could read him too easily. When he slowly opened the door, the light from the fireplace was more than enough for his unnatural eyesight. Closing the door, he moved on silent feet to the bed.

Sprawled on his back across the mattress, Kevin was oblivious to his watcher. Gentle snores punctuated his sleep while the covers, bunched at his waist, revealed his broad chest.

Lorcan's hungry gaze roamed over the wide shoulders, the fair skin and the small rosy nipples before he pulled up the blanket. The room was warm enough, but it hid temptation.

Lorcan's heightened sense of smell caught the fragrant traces of herbal shampoo. He couldn't resist running his fingers through Kevin's bright blond tresses, still damp from the shower. The scent transferred to Lorcan's fingers. Bringing them to his lips, he feathered them over his mouth. A small groan escaped.

He wanted to bury his face in the young man's hair, feel the strength of the hard body against him. The desire to mark Kevin, drink from him, taste him, was powerful. The itch of his gums warned Lorcan he should leave. The need to feed was strong and looking at him made it worse. Lorcan forced himself to turn away.

"Hello…"

The whispered word took Lorcan by surprise. "I…I'm sorry. I didn't mean to wake you." He turned back. The deep blue eyes peering at him in the darkness sent a sharp tremor of desire through him.

"It's okay. I need to thank you. I have a little money. For…for the food, the room…"

"You don't need to pay me." Lorcan knew he should excuse himself and leave but he couldn't resist. Perching on the edge of the bed, he risked the temptation. "You don't owe me anything."

"You stopped them…"

If Lorcan's hearing hadn't been keen, he wouldn't have heard the whispered words. "I couldn't let them hurt you."

"You could have been hurt—or worse."

"Not likely. They were bullies and cowards. Confronted, their kind always scatter. I wish I could have kept you from being injured."

"It could have…would have been worse, if you hadn't." Kevin bit his lip, a frown wrinkling his forehead. "I could…you know…" Kevin's hand moved across the blankets to Lorcan's thigh as the young man's gaze darted toward Lorcan's groin.

Lorcan's fantasy of Kevin's mouth wrapped around his dick flashed through his mind. Shuddering in the darkness, he hoped the young man wouldn't be able to see it, feel it. He was desperate to take Kevin up on his offer but he shouldn't.

Intending to push the hand away, his hand held Kevin's instead. "It's not necessary. You don't have to do anything you don't want to."

"And if I want to..." The voice trailed off. The darkness couldn't hide the heat of the blush spreading across Kevin's face and chest.

Lorcan couldn't think of an answer. Rational thought was no longer possible. The touch of Kevin's hand sent searing heat through his thigh, straight to his groin. His fingers tightened on Kevin's as Lorcan's breathing changed to panting. With his mind screaming warnings of past loss, he leaned toward Kevin, toward the full lips, the fragrant hair, the broad chest. The slight flare of desire in Kevin's eyes was all he needed to drown out the dark memories for now.

Lorcan's lips brushed Kevin's gently. The warm mouth moved a hesitant welcome under his as he pressed closer. He nibbled at the full lower lip, feeling Kevin's mouth begin to nip back. The moment seemed to last forever.

Lorcan groaned as a hesitant tongue brushed against his mouth. His own tongue moved to catch the retreating moist heat. Kevin's arms snaked around his neck as their kiss deepened. Without losing the exquisite contact, Lorcan moved until he lay half across the younger man.

Reacting to the lean muscles and masculine planes of the body below him, his cock filled fast, aching with desires so long denied. Lorcan's fingers tangled in the long blond hair as his tongue explored the moist, willing depths of Kevin's mouth.

Soft moans vibrated against his lips as Kevin's arms tightened around his neck.

Lorcan released his hold on Kevin's hair to push the covers down, tracing the outside of Kevin's thigh on the way back up. Rolling to his side, his hand tugged at Kevin's leg until the younger man faced him, the slim, toned limb draped over Lorcan's hip.

Kevin's obvious arousal brushed against his own erection through the silk of Lorcan's robe. His hand slid around to caress Kevin's ass before pulling him hard against the length of his body. Their lips locked in hungry bliss. A gentle thrust of Kevin's hips made Lorcan gasp.

"Oh yes..." Lorcan hadn't had this in so long. Making love to someone instead of using them, lingering kisses instead of a means to a meal. His desire for Kevin's mouth around his cock faded as the need to touch, to taste, to explore, the younger man overwhelmed him.

Lorcan's fingers trailed across the sweet ass, feathered strokes lingering at the cleft of his cheeks. The younger man's muscles tightened as Lorcan's fingers slid along the tempting valley toward his puckered hole.

Kevin pressed hard into Lorcan, as if to avoid the searching fingers. A muffled moan of protest escaped the younger man's throat, his lips stilling as Lorcan's fingers found what they were seeking.

Lorcan teased with gentle strokes but didn't try to penetrate. The memory of the young man's fear in the alley stayed in the back of his mind. Long moments passed before the rigid body relaxed and the soft lips returned to life, matching the fervor of his own.

Trailing his fingers over Kevin's tight ass and hip, Lorcan moved his hand between them. The younger man's body arched as Lorcan grasped his cock. Hard and hot and everything Lorcan thought it would be, everything he wanted it to be. He stroked the searing flesh with long, steady movements as Kevin moaned into his kisses. Lorcan's thumb slid over the tip, gathering the moisture pooling there, smearing it around the velvet crown.

Kevin's body trembled and when Lorcan pushed him onto his back, Kevin didn't hesitate. His face was a picture of wonder and desire. The full lips were swollen from kisses and the deep blue eyes glazed with a passion mirroring Lorcan's own. The hint of trust there thrilled Lorcan almost as much as his desire.

Lorcan couldn't stop his smile as he kissed his way down Kevin's throat. The scent of the sweet crimson nectar pulsing through the vein teased him as his lips nibbled at the tender skin. As the younger man arched against his mouth, a rush of thirst threatened to consume him. His fangs itched to slide free of their sheaths, to sink into the pale flesh. He forced his mind, his body, not to react to his hunger. First, a different appetite demanded quenching. His hand moved down Kevin's taut stomach to his swollen erection. The urge to taste his hot, leaking cock overwhelmed even the need for blood.

Moving past the lure of Kevin's neck, Lorcan nibbled his way down the smooth chest until his tongue found an already hardened nipple. Kevin's body arched up off the bed as Lorcan suckled the tiny nubbin of flesh. He stroked the hard shaft as he continued to torment the younger man's chest. His own cock throbbed with need. Lorcan pressed his aching flesh against Kevin's thigh, his leg hooking over the other man's leg, rubbing against him.

"Oh God," Kevin moaned as Lorcan moved to the other nipple. "I...I..."

"What, Kevin?" Lorcan asked between a lick and a nibble. "What do you want?"

"I should be doing... I should... I owe you..."

Lorcan moved back to Kevin's lips. "You can't possibly realize how much I want this." He devoured Kevin's mouth, kissing him hard and deep, relishing the rough stubble against his face.

Lorcan had almost forgotten the little things. Making love to a man after so many years of self-denial drove him almost to the edge of reason. Lifting his head to gaze into the liquid blue eyes, Lorcan murmured, "You don't owe me but if you did, this is all the payment I need."

Kevin's hands pulled Lorcan's head down, kissing him with bruising force.

Lorcan didn't miss the hint of moisture in Kevin's eyes right before their lips met. The vulnerability, the sadness in the younger man tugged at his heart. But Kevin's frantic body against him, pushing his cock against Lorcan's body, distracted him from further speculation.

Lorcan grinned against Kevin's lips. "Slow down, Kevin. We have all night."

The younger man's body slowed its frenzied movement to small thrusts as Lorcan once again explored his lips. Slow, lazy exploration turned to hungry mouthing. As much as Lorcan wanted to maintain his hold on Kevin's mouth, so much more was there to explore. In spite of his admonition to Kevin, Lorcan didn't want to wait all night to taste the younger man. With nipping kisses, he pulled away, leaving Kevin panting for air.

Rising slowly to his knees, Lorcan opened his robe, the silk rustling with a liquid sound as it slid off the bed.

Lorcan admired the view in front of him. Kevin was beautiful. No other word fit so well. His shoulder-length blond hair spread across the pillow. His pale skin glowed golden in the soft firelight. The well-toned, almost hairless chest wasn't overly muscled but enough to show he worked at it. The narrow waist drew Lorcan's gaze to the soft blond hair starting below the navel and thickening as it trailed lower. The hard cock was impressive in size and girth, nicely veined and weeping with arousal.

It would be so easy to fall for him, drown in the pools of deep blue expectation staring back. A niggling thought warned him, reminding him of the sorrow of loss, but he brushed it aside.

Lorcan moved to kneel between the young man's long legs. His hands skimmed across Kevin's stomach and up to his chest. A gentle tweak to the tiny, hard nipples then his fingers traced back down to the narrow hips. One hand grasped the dripping cock and Lorcan leaned over.

His tongue dipped into the wet slit, tasting the bitter nectar pooled there. Kevin's fingers twisted in the sheets as Lorcan suckled the velvet head. A strangled moan sounded as Lorcan swallowed the hard flesh to the base. He could taste a fresh gush of liquid as he moved back up to the crown.

"You taste so good," Lorcan murmured.

Scooting down to lie nestled between Kevin's thighs, Lorcan's aching cock pushed into the mattress, seeking relief in the pressure. He laved the length of Kevin's dick, mapping every vein, each contour of the hard shaft on the journey down until he reached the tight balls. Lorcan's tongue prodded the sensitive sac before he sucked one into his mouth with gentle care, exploring the wrinkled texture and the musky taste.

One finger traced a path down to the perineum, pausing to massage it. Kevin writhed on the bed as Lorcan released the tightening sac and his tongue followed his finger. Lorcan paused to slip his index finger in his mouth to wet it. His tongue returned to prod Kevin's sensitive spot as his finger found the tight puckered anus.

"No..."

Lorcan looked up to see fear in Kevin's eyes. "I won't hurt you."

A rush of emotion flowed through him as Kevin's terror faded to hesitant trust. His gaze stayed locked with Kevin's as Lorcan pushed his finger slowly past the tight ring. His languid tongue moved up Kevin's cock as his finger searched the tight, velvet-lined passage for the prostate. Lorcan grinned as Kevin's eyes rolled back in his head. He'd found it.

"Oh God," Kevin sighed as Lorcan swallowed the silken head once more. His finger pushed against the hard knot of Kevin's prostate with the same rhythm Lorcan's mouth moved on the overheated flesh. A fresh gush of bitter taste signaled his impending orgasm to Lorcan.

"Yes, oh yes…" Kevin's breathless moans forewarned him as well.

Frantic hips arched as Lorcan tasted the first spurt of thick, bitter fluid. His hand grasped the jerking flesh and milked it as his mouth moved to suck the inside of Kevin's thigh. His eager fangs shot out and sank into the quivering flesh, into the large vein beneath the surface.

As the sweet taste of blood mingled with Kevin's pungent juices on his tongue, Lorcan's own orgasm erupted into the bedding. He drank deeply of the sweet crimson elixir as his moans mingled with Kevin's. The rush of orgasm and blood overwhelmed him until the rapid cooling of Kevin's body caused his overeager fangs to retract in fear.

"Damn," Lorcan muttered, rolling off the bed. He pulled the covers up over Kevin's now unconscious body. "Tomas!"

Lorcan stalked to the door, heedless of his nakedness. Yanking it open, he yelled again. "Tomas!"

The older man moved with a speed that belied his age.

"I drank too much. We've got to keep him from going into shock."

Chapter Four
ಬಿ

Grogginess filled Kevin's mind as he woke, confused at the unfamiliar surroundings until his memory kicked in. His whole body blushed as last night's activities flowed into his mind in vivid recall. His fingers traced his still bruised lips as he thought about the passion his dark lover's touch, his kisses, had roused. The whole encounter seemed like a dream. Kevin never thought the scrape of stubble, the hard body of a man, would be so sensual. His sexual experience with men had been limited to giving blowjobs, not receiving them.

Kevin didn't have much more experience with women. His family standing aside, he had always been shy. His stepfather had done a very good job at killing his self-confidence and that fact showed in his relationships. Or was something else causing his relationships with women to fail...

The thought of the dark-haired man's lips on his body sent blood rushing through him. The knowing hands had brought him to a peak he had never experienced. The idea of his touching him again caused his heart to beat faster. Even the intruding finger hadn't dampened the sensuous fever that had racked his body.

And the kisses... Kevin had never kissed a man before. The raspy scrape of a masculine jaw against his, the hard lips kissing him with rough thoroughness, sent shivers through him. Kevin hadn't known making love with a man could feel so good.

His mind raced at the idea. The man had made love to him. So different from his recent encounters, hidden in the dark, a dick in Kevin's mouth, sour fluids gagging him. No money tossed dismissively at him for services rendered. What happened last night was tender, almost loving.

Kevin wondered where the dark-haired man was now. Would the taste of his benefactor's cock seem different considering the pleasure Kevin found in his arms, in his mouth?

Kevin's body ached and the blankets couldn't keep the chill from his bones. He hadn't felt this bad yesterday. Alone in the bed, he finally noticed Tomas dozing in a chair nearby.

With a slight jerk of his body, Tomas' eyes opened. "You're awake. Good." The man's voice had a puzzling tone of relief. "I'll get Lorcan." And then he was gone.

"Lorcan..." Kevin whispered the word. He hadn't known his rescuer's name. Even though it wasn't the first time he'd let a stranger use him for sex, somehow knowing the man's name made him feel less like a whore.

"Kevin?" Lorcan entered the room quietly.

The concern in Lorcan's eyes made it difficult for Kevin to keep his emotions under control. It didn't help when Lorcan sat on the edge of the bed and stroked his hair. He touched him as a lover, not a trick.

"I'm sorry..." Kevin began.

"There's nothing to be sorry for. You weren't strong enough for... Well, for what we ended up doing." Lorcan's grin was infectious.

"I passed out?" The grin teasing Kevin's lips faded. The heat of his embarrassment spread across his face. "I didn't...I mean, you didn't...you know... Get anything back." Never had he come so hard. Kevin shouldn't be surprised he'd lost consciousness but it meant he'd left Lorcan high and dry.

The musical laugh of the man surprised him. "Don't worry about it! I received plenty. The bedding had to be changed around you."

Kevin ducked his head and closed his eyes as the heat of the man's stare sent a shudder of arousal through him. A puff of breath on his face made him open his eyes as Lorcan's lips touched his. In spite of the weakness in his body, his cock took interest at the contact.

His mouth opened to the gentle pressure. Hot, moist flesh slipped past Kevin's lips and met his tongue. A discreet knock at the door interrupted them before Kevin could find out how weak he really was.

"Come in," Lorcan called. His fingers ran across Kevin's cheek and lips before he moved away from the bed to greet Tomas.

Lorcan was glad to see a little color return to Kevin's face. Too much blood loss and he would have to send for medical help. A situation difficult to explain. The few times Lorcan had screwed up before, he'd had to leave the victim at an emergency room.

He didn't want to risk it with Kevin, didn't want him to leave yet. Or maybe ever.

Tomas waited with a tray as Lorcan helped Kevin to a sitting position.

Placing pillows behind him for support, Lorcan couldn't resist planting a soft kiss on his forehead. Somehow the younger man brought out emotions Lorcan had deliberately suppressed for so long he thought he'd lost the capability to feel them. Protectiveness collided with tenderness and the desire to keep him close.

Stepping back, Lorcan allowed Tomas to set the bed tray across Kevin's lap. His old friend made a quick escape, leaving Lorcan to tend to Kevin himself. Sitting carefully on the edge of the bed so as not to disturb the tray, Lorcan removed the cover on the bowl. Kevin's bewildered look caused his lips to curve into a grin. "You need to regain your strength, so you need to eat."

"But you don't have to wait on me." The pampering clearly confused Kevin.

"But I want to." Lorcan's smile seemed to reassure him since the tension in Kevin's shoulders and neck relaxed. "I want to take care of you." Lorcan surprised himself with the admission.

Kevin could hardly keep his fingers around the spoon. His first shaky attempt ended with liquid dripping down his chin. "Uh, sorry…"

Lorcan just grinned. Wiping Kevin's chin with a napkin, he removed the spoon from his fingers. "Let me."

Kevin wanted to hide under the covers as Lorcan held the full spoon against his mouth. The rich flavor of beef burst on his tongue as he sipped the hot liquid carefully. "Do you live here alone?" Kevin asked, his curiosity overcoming his embarrassment.

"Just me and Tomas. He's worked for my family for a long time so he's more family than servant."

"What kind of work do you do?" Kevin opened his mouth for more soup.

"Import-export business. A family business for hundreds of years. MacKenna Enterprises. It started out as the MacKenna Trading Company in the mid-1700s. I really don't have a lot to do with the day-to-day running of the company. What about you?"

Kevin lowered his eyes from the inquisitive look on Lorcan's face. What about him? How could he explain his life? A child of wealth and privilege reduced to sucking cocks in alleys. Not a pretty picture. Kevin wasn't sure he wanted to explain it. Glancing up at Lorcan's green eyes, he found only understanding.

Lorcan offered the pale young man another taste of soup. His curiosity gnawed but he didn't press Kevin for answers. When Kevin decided to tell him, he would. Lorcan wanted nothing to scare this man away. For the first time in a long while, something stirred in Lorcan's lonely heart.

Was it Kevin's vulnerability? Was it his innocence?

Lorcan wasn't sure, but he wanted to find out. He wanted to know more about the man who had already wormed his way past Lorcan's defenses and touched his heart.

"You said you had an audition?"

Kevin snorted amusement. "Yeah, kind of. My agent is supposed to set it up."

Lorcan chuckled as he lifted the spoon again. "Not a very good agent?"

"I don't know. Maybe I'm just not a very good actor." He sipped the offered soup.

"How long have you been acting?"

Kevin's eyes stared at something not in the room. "All my life…" He shook his head and returned to the present. "I've been trying for three years, since I came to New York. Before that mostly college stuff."

"Where are you from?"

"D.C.—Washington."

"Nice place. I haven't been there in years though." Another spoonful. "Do you have family there?"

Kevin swallowed before answering. "My mother and my stepfather." His eyes closed as his brow wrinkled.

The sadness and pain in his expression kept Lorcan from asking any more questions. Lorcan wanted to know more but he'd heard enough for now. Somehow, he'd keep Kevin near. He would have to be careful though, Kevin couldn't know the darkness surrounding Lorcan's life. Not yet. He wanted—no, needed—to bind Kevin to him without letting the young man know his true nature.

A huge yawn split Kevin's face.

Though only half the broth was gone, Lorcan removed the tray. "Lie back," he said as he stood. "You should get more rest."

As Kevin sank into the pillows, he breathed a huge sigh.

After depositing the tray on the table, Lorcan pulled the covers over him and sat on the edge of the bed. His fingers traced Kevin's hairline before his hand came to rest on his cheek.

Kevin's fingers wrapped around Lorcan's wrist and a whisper of a kiss touched his palm. "Stay." The blue eyes emphasized the almost inaudible word.

Lorcan's hand moved enough for his thumb to trace a line across Kevin's full bottom lip. Nodding, he stood and stripped off his shirt and jeans, leaving him in his underwear.

Slipping under the covers, Lorcan soon found his arms full of a hard muscled body. Fragrant hair tickled his chest as Kevin's head found its way there. A lean leg slid over his and a cool foot hooked under his knee. At peace for the first time in so long, Lorcan breathed whispered kisses on the fragrant hair. His eyes stung with emotion as Kevin's breath evened out. He would stay for a little while longer.

Lorcan wouldn't make the same mistake with Kevin as he had with Gustave. However, perhaps Kevin could help keep the loneliness at bay. And in return, Lorcan could keep Kevin safe.

*****

Frantic cries and a thrashing body woke Lorcan from his dreamless slumber. Lorcan's arms tightened around Kevin as the nightmare held him in its grasp.

With a choked gasp, Kevin awakened. Once recognition lit his eyes, he moved to bury his face in Lorcan's neck, his chest pressed hard against Lorcan's, rising and falling with rapid breaths.

"It's okay," Lorcan whispered in Kevin's ear. He planted gentle kisses on the distraught man's temple. "It was just a nightmare. I've got you. It's okay now."

His voice drove Kevin deeper into his arms. Muffled words slowly became distinguishable. "I can't believe I did that. It was so stupid but I needed cash fast."

Lorcan closed his eyes in sympathy at the pain in Kevin's words. "Let me help," he whispered. "I have plenty of money. I can help you." The offer came out without thought. Something about Kevin lowered his guard and opened his heart.

Kevin's body stiffened against him.

"You don't have to do anything. Last night was…was incredible but not necessary. I have more money than I know what to do with. If I can help, I want to."

Kevin's arms tightened around Lorcan almost to the point of pain. With the young man's weakened condition, the strength of Kevin's grip surprised Lorcan.

Lorcan stroked his back gently. "You could stay here or I can help you with your rent or whatever expenses you have. Where you sleep doesn't matter." It did matter. Lorcan wanted Kevin close but he would accept his decision if the trembling young man refused. As long as Kevin let him help, Lorcan wouldn't push him into staying here.

Lorcan held him close as words flowed from Kevin.

"My father died when I was seven. My stepfather… My mother married him three years later. He didn't like me. Always telling me what a screw-up I was. Most of the time, I tried to be good but it didn't seem to matter…" Kevin's voice trailed off.

"It's okay, Kevin. You don't have to talk about it." Lorcan's blood heated at the thought of Kevin's stepfather mistreating a child. "He can't hurt you now."

"I know it's unreasonable to fear him now but sometimes I... He's powerful and has a lot of influential friends. The nightmares..." With a deep sigh, Kevin relaxed in Lorcan's arms. "Sometimes it seems so real..."

"Doesn't matter who he is, I won't let him hurt you." He had his own ways of dealing with a threat.

"If he found out what I've been doing... You know, with men, for money. I don't know what he would do. If anyone found out the great Senator Chandler's stepson was... Well, it could ruin him." Kevin lifted his head and his eyes met Lorcan's in the dim light. "But I needed the money. Mother used to send me money once in a while. I didn't really like taking it but it came in handy for the extra stuff. I even kept track. Planned to pay her back. But Walter found out and made her stop."

"What kind of extra stuff?" Lorcan never paid much attention to the acting profession. His life was one long drama. Why bother.

"Nice clothes for auditions, photos for my portfolio, acting lessons." Kevin snorted his disgust. "I came here to be an actor. Turns out, I'm probably a better waiter. But I love acting. It's like an addiction. I've only had a few parts here and there. A couple of local commercials, some walk-on roles off-Broadway." Kevin laughed against Lorcan's chest. "Off-off-off-Broadway." Kevin pulled away from Lorcan's arms and rolled over to lie on his back. "But there's something about it... Anyway, between the few parts I get and my job as a waiter, I make enough to keep a roof over my head but it's not enough for much else."

The sound of Kevin's nails dragging through the rough beard made Lorcan glance over at him.

"When Mother stopped sending the extra cash, well, I got by. New York is an expensive city. But I cut out the nonessentials and worked extra shifts when I could get them. I even managed to save a little money. It made life more difficult but I could deal with it. Until this latest audition…"

"Why this one?"

"It was a closed audition and my agent wouldn't put my name in the hat until I got new head shots, photos for my portfolio… He'd been after me for a while to do it and I know I needed new ones but they're really expensive. I used up what little I had saved and still came up short. With less than a week before the casting call, I got desperate. And stupid… I thought about calling my mother, asking for a loan. But Walter started tracking her calls after he found out about the money. I didn't want him mad at her. So instead… Well, you know."

A sharp laugh surprised Lorcan.

"In another three years, it won't make a difference what the old SOB does or doesn't do."

"Why three years?"

"I'll be thirty. My real father left me a trust fund. I'll be able to get my mother out of there and take care of her myself. I just hope I can convince her to leave him. I guess I should have played Walter's game and done something else in the meantime."

"So there's nothing else you can do? What about college?" The sound of a gentle snort made Lorcan turn on his side to watch Kevin's profile.

"I wanted to study drama. Walter refused to pay for it. So like the stubborn asshole I am, I tried to do it on my own. Financial aid said my family made too much money so I waited tables, drove a pizza delivery car, anything, but I could only afford a few classes at a time. Instead of taking anything useful, I concentrated on all the drama classes I could. I finally quit when I was twenty-four and came here."

"There's nothing wrong with stubborn pride."

"There is when you end up on your knees in an alley..." Kevin bit his lip as the muscles in his throat worked hard against a swallow. "Oh God, if Walter found out about the men... He'd blame my mother. Say it was her fault like everything else I did. It wouldn't matter that I'm not gay."

"I'm sorry..." Guilt caused Lorcan's breath to catch. He hadn't realized Kevin wasn't gay. "Last night... I shouldn't have..."

"No!"

Kevin's vehemence startled him.

"I wanted..." As he turned to face Lorcan, his voice turned softer. "I wanted you," he whispered.

Lorcan caressed the pale face, running his thumb across the now softer growth of beard to the full lips. "And I wanted you as I haven't wanted anyone in more years than you'd believe."

And Lorcan wanted him now, more than before. He willed his body not to react to Kevin's nearness. He didn't want to frighten him. Somehow, he would find a way to keep Kevin with him.

A shiver ran through Lorcan's body as Kevin's lips formed the hint of a kiss against his thumb. Lorcan's eyes half closed as a warm, moist tongue flickered against it.

Considering his weakened state from blood loss, Kevin pushed with a strength that surprised Lorcan. He rolled over on his back as Kevin's body covered him.

"Kevin," he moaned. "You need to rest." Lorcan's body was rebelling. His cock began to swell as Kevin moved his hips against Lorcan's.

"Please...I want you." Kevin's whispered plea crashed through his willpower.

Lorcan's hips moved to meet Kevin's shy thrust.

Kevin's body trembled against him. The younger man responded to the slow, grinding movement.

Winding his fingers through Kevin's hair, Lorcan pulled his face down until their lips met. Soft kisses, tentative nibbles then lazy tongues. Kevin's moan matched Lorcan's as their bodies undulated in slow waves, stoking the fire deep in Lorcan's groin.

The sigh Lorcan exhaled when Kevin's mouth left his transformed into a gasp as full lips moved down to Lorcan's neck. His head lolled back and his fingers loosened their grip on Kevin's hair. Sweet kisses moved along his throat, the new growth of beard leaving a tickling trail. A whimpered protest didn't keep Kevin's body from moving off him.

Soon, the hungry mouth moved down to Lorcan's chest. His fingers still tangled in Kevin's hair tightened as a hot mouth descended on a sensitive nipple. Panting gasps exploded from Lorcan as teeth raked the hard nub of flesh. A hesitant hand slid down his stomach to rest near his hard, aching cock.

"Yes," Lorcan breathed. "Touch me. Please."

Lorcan almost came when a timid hand pressed against the tight cotton boxers, cupping him with cautious heat. His hips pushed his cock up into Kevin's palm. Wet lips captured Lorcan's other nipple, sucking hard.

"Oh shit," he moaned. His body jerked hard as pleasure coursed through him.

Cool air replaced the warmth of Kevin's hand. Lorcan opened his eyes as inquisitive fingers teased the elastic at the top of his boxers. Heat slid under the waistband and engulfed his cock. Lorcan pushed hard into Kevin's hand. An unintelligible cry from Lorcan accompanied the thrust.

Kevin's mouth moved lower, his tongue licking a trail of heat down Lorcan's stomach.

Cool air chilled the path in a sensuous contrast. A rush of air teased the crown of his dick as Kevin pushed Lorcan's boxers down over his erection.

Kneeling over him, Kevin's face flushed as he licked his lips.

Lorcan didn't know if arousal or fear sent the blood rushing through the young man's face. A look of frightened determination crossed Kevin's features.

"Kevin, you don't have to…"

A puff of heated breath signaled Kevin's determination seconds before his hot mouth circled the tip.

Lorcan's words trailed off as he barely controlled the need to thrust into the moist cavern.

Gentle sucking accompanied Kevin's curious tongue. His inexperience was obvious but also erotic in a way.

That alone almost made Lorcan explode. He was the first man Kevin wanted out of desire not necessity. "Feels so good," Lorcan whispered. His fingers combed through the long strands of hair as the hot mouth bobbed on his cock in slow, cautious strokes.

One hand circled the base, moving slowly up and down Lorcan's aching flesh as Kevin sucked. The soft tongue moved with deliberate movements as if unsure of its purpose.

Lorcan wouldn't last much longer. The tightness in his balls and the ache in the pit of his stomach were too intense. "Kevin," Lorcan whispered. Gentle tugs at the long blond hair attempted to warn him. "I'm going to come." His breath grew ragged as Kevin's mouth sucked harder, faster. A moan resonated through his cock. The vibrations were the last straw. "Oh yes," Lorcan yelled as his body pulsed with pleasure.

In spite of the slight gagging at first, Kevin's mouth continued sucking, drinking him, stroking and milking him. The younger man released him with an exhausted sigh then buried his face in Lorcan's groin.

His orgasm blocked out the world as his vision blurred and lights danced before his eyes. Lorcan's sense of hearing came back first. The rapid heartbeat of his lover, the rushing of the blood pulsing through his veins caught his attention. Concern for the younger man brushed aside the residual glow of Lorcan's ecstasy.

Once again he had placed his own physical needs over Kevin's health. Lorcan should have stopped him. Kevin was still too weak from blood loss. He sat up, reaching for him. Pulling Kevin's almost limp body up so his head rested on the pillows, Lorcan yanked the blankets over them. He ran a hand over the covers, smoothing them.

A small moan lodged in Kevin's throat as Lorcan encountered the man's hard erection. In spite of his obvious exhaustion, Kevin was still aroused.

Lorcan slid his hand under the covers and found the hot flesh weeping with desire. Holding Kevin close, Lorcan's lips wandered his face as his hand stroked Kevin's hot cock with firm, experienced strokes.

"You felt so good, Kevin," Lorcan whispered as he kissed Kevin's ear. "So good."

Kevin's body jerked, reacting to the tight grip around his cock.

"Relax. It's my turn to make you feel good."

Kevin's body relaxed against him.

Covering Kevin's mouth with slow, hungry kisses, Lorcan stroked his young lover. Kevin's willing lips opened. The taste of his own semen lingered as Lorcan's tongue explored the warm, wet heaven.

Kevin's hand moved to stroke Lorcan's hair as his mouth submitted to the deep kiss. Soft moans mingled as Kevin's body arched into the rhythm of Lorcan's strokes. "Lorcan—" Kevin's cry accompanied the jerking of his hips.

Adjusting his movements to Kevin's, Lorcan's hand increased the pace. His mouth locked with his young lover's lips as warm liquid coated his fingers. When an anguished sound interrupted their kiss, Lorcan drew back.

"Oh damn, did I hurt you?" Wiping his hand on the top blanket, he wrapped his arms around Kevin.

"Not hurt." Kevin buried his face in Lorcan's chest, muffling his words. "Not hurt. Not you."

"Then what's wrong? Let me fix it." Lorcan stroked Kevin's strong back.

"You can't."

"Let me try." Lorcan's own feelings surprised him.

"I wish I could go back. Start over."

"What do you mean?"

"I never knew I could feel this way. I…I feel so… What I did before, with other men. I wish it would go away. That it was only like this." The last sentence faded to a whisper.

"I can't change the past. If I could, I would. But I can help you to forget." Lorcan nuzzled the soft hair. "Sleep…"

The memory of Gustave's dark eyes warned Lorcan. He knew he was already in over his head. He wanted to keep his new lover close. No matter the cost.

Chapter Five
ಞ

Kevin slipped on his new jeans. Lorcan had insisted on buying him new clothes. The act of giving seemed to give Loran pleasure so Kevin hadn't objected too much. Besides, except for his audition clothes, most of his were almost threadbare. Three years of wearing them tended to do that. But the few new things he bought, he saved for interviews and auditions.

Of course, Lorcan had picked these out. He had insisted Kevin stay in the apartment until he was stronger. His lover was so concerned about his health. But tonight they were going out. Well, at least to Kevin's apartment to get his few belongings.

Nearly a week had passed since the incident in the alley. Kevin couldn't believe so much had changed in such a short span of time. For the first time in so long, Kevin felt wanted. Not since his mother married Walter. Giving in to Lorcan's desire to stay here had been easy. Kevin was willing to give in to a lot more of Lorcan's desires and wanted to explore some of his own. He couldn't keep his hands off the dark man, touching him, running his fingers through the dark curly hair.

They had only made love twice. The last few nights Lorcan had insisted Kevin rest and conserve his strength. Kevin felt much better. The strange weakness from his first day here wasn't completely gone. Too much activity drained him pretty fast but three square meals a day and a lot of sleep did wonders for the body. In equal measures, Lorcan soothed his soul.

Kevin had never, in his wildest dreams, thought having a hard male body pressed against his while he slept could be so comforting. In his hidden fantasies, he only thought of sex, not the gentleness afterward. Lorcan, in spite of his ban against sex, had stayed the last two nights—or days. His days and nights were backward.

Lorcan was a night owl. He said most of his business dealings were overseas so he had gotten in the habit of keeping hours to match other countries. That fact didn't matter. All that mattered was Lorcan's body next to him as he drifted off to sleep.

A slight knock sounded before the door opened. Lorcan's smile greeted him. "You ready?"

"Yeah, almost," Kevin said as he finished tying his sneakers. "Now I am!" He grinned as he stood. The pale blue cashmere sweater was soft and wonderful against his skin. He thought he must look pretty good in it and the tight jeans. Lorcan's eyes were full of lust as they raked him up and down. "You like?"

Lorcan exhaled a sharp breath. "I love!"

A shiver of desire ran through him. "We could, you know..." Kevin's head tilted toward the bed. "One for the road?" he said with a suggestive arch of his eyebrows.

Lorcan laughed at his eager lover and wrapped his arms around the younger man. Kevin stood a little taller than Lorcan but not enough to hamper his kisses.

Kevin's arms snaked around Lorcan's neck as his body pressed against his lover.

Soft kisses, the hard body, made the temptation great but so close to the time to feed, Lorcan wasn't sure he could control the urge. Besides, he wasn't sure he wanted to drink from him yet. The more his emotions became involved, the more the desire to be honest grew. "We should take care of this now," Lorcan said, suppressing his body's needs and desires. "I already have men meeting us there to move your things."

Kevin shook his head with a regretful smile. "Oh well. I don't know why you think I have tons of stuff to move. There's really not much."

"I know, but you're still weak, Tomas is old and I'm lazy!" Lorcan laughed. "We'll let someone else do the grunt work." He held out his hand to his now-chuckling partner. The warm hand in his reassured Lorcan. He wanted Kevin to be comfortable with him in every way.

* * * * *

With his arm tight around Kevin in the backseat of the limo, Lorcan didn't miss the shiver from Kevin as they drove past the alley where his attack occurred. Lorcan kissed his forehead and gave him a quick squeeze of reassurance. "Hey, we wouldn't have met if things had been different."

"I know. I don't think I would still be alive if you hadn't been there."

Lorcan shuddered at the idea. The thought of losing him was unbearable. He knew he would someday, but not now, not for a long time.

The limo stopped in front of a rundown four-story building. Originally the building housed a business on the first floor and three apartments above, one on each floor. Someone had remodeled it to fit four tiny apartments per floor. The business on the first floor was an adult video store with offers of peep shows and live sex acts. Not the best of neighborhoods.

Three men stood near a van. One walked toward the limo as Tomas climbed out of the front passenger seat. They spoke a few words and then Tomas opened the back door for Lorcan and Kevin.

"Sir," Tomas said formally, playing up the part of servant for the three strangers. "We can go up without you if you'd like. There's no need for you to climb four flights of stairs."

Kevin squeezed his hand. "I want to go," he whispered. "I have some things hidden. I can go alone."

That wasn't happening. "We'll be all right, Tomas. Lead the way."

The driver stayed with the vehicles as the three men followed Tomas, Lorcan and Kevin. Lorcan kept a strong arm around his lover's waist, afraid he was still too weak from the severe blood loss to make the climb. He was correct in his assumption. By the time they started up the last flight of stairs, Kevin's muscles trembled under his arm.

Lorcan paused on the landing between flights. "Are you okay? We can rest for a minute."

"No, let's get this over with."

Lorcan nodded for the three men to go in front of them before he helped Kevin up the remaining stairs. The stench in the stairwell was repugnant to Lorcan's sensitive nose. He couldn't stand the idea of Kevin living like this. Lorcan would make sure he never did again.

The apartment door was open when they finally reached the top of the stairs. The tiny area was neat but the apartment smelled of age and disrepair. A leaking radiator left water stains on the floor and the paint curled in strips down the walls.

"I'm sorry, you should have stayed downstairs," Kevin murmured.

His embarrassment showed in the slumped shoulders and the rising blush on his lover's face. Lorcan reached for the downcast chin and lifted his face so he could look in Kevin's eyes.

"You have nothing to apologize for. Just get the things you want. Anything you don't want, we'll have them throw out." He leaned in with a brief brush of lips against Kevin's. His hearing caught the slight snort of disgust from one of the men Tomas had hired. With a defiant look toward the culprit, he pulled Kevin into a tight hug. The guilty party turned from the glare in Lorcan's eyes. "Get your things and let's go."

* * * * *

Kevin's hidden treasures turned out to be two pictures. One was of his father and mother, the other a family portrait taken the month before his father died. Lorcan smiled at the child in the photo. His innocence and vulnerability still showed in the man he had become. He also had a stash of a little cash, all hidden in an envelope taped under a battered dresser. His other belongings consisted of two fairly nice pairs of slacks and shirts—his audition clothes, he called them—and some other threadbare casual clothes. The few ragged towels and washcloths and bedding went in a box destined for a homeless shelter nearby.

Lorcan helped Kevin down the stairs in the wake of the three hired men. A second trip wasn't necessary. Kevin's meager belongings easily fit in three boxes. They took a while to navigate the stairs. Kevin shouldn't have made the climb in the first place.

Finally, the end was in sight. Cold air rushed into the hall as Tomas opened the door. Once outside, Lorcan noticed one of the helpers talking to the limo driver. When the man turned, he recognized the same one who'd shown disgust earlier.

"Tomas, find out what they talked about."

* * * * *

Lorcan closed the door of Kevin's room softly. He had fallen asleep in the car. Once in his bed, only a few minutes elapsed before he was out again. Lorcan leaned against the door and glanced down the hallway. He needed to find Tomas, to ask him what the limo driver said to the man helping them. Something didn't feel right. It could be the homophobic attitude of the man but Lorcan wasn't taking any chances. His instinct said something was wrong and he had survived many years by listening to it.

Tomas appeared in the hall with a tray for Kevin.

Lorcan shook his head. "He's asleep. It was probably too soon for him to be exerting himself. The stairs did him in." Lorcan headed for the study with a motion of his head for Tomas to follow.

Tomas set the tray on a table then stirred the fire as Lorcan slid into a chair.

"So what did the driver say?"

Tomas settled in the chair near the table. He pulled the cover off the tray and grabbed some grapes. "Nothing much." He popped a grape in his mouth and stared at the fire.

Lorcan knew better than to rush him.

"Basically wanted to know who you were, who Kevin was. What you were doing in the neighborhood. Seems those were popular questions tonight. The driver said another man approached him as well." Tomas popped another grape in his mouth and chewed thoughtfully. His eyes lifted from the fire and met Lorcan's gaze. "Do you think Kevin's in danger?"

It shouldn't have surprised Lorcan to hear his own fears from Tomas' mouth.

"I don't know." Lorcan's gaze dropped from Tomas'. "I love him." The words jumped from his lips on their own.

"I know."

"I need to feed. I can't...I can't do it again without telling him." Just talking about it made Lorcan's hunger intensify.

"I can arrange something, somewhere."

Lorcan looked up at Tomas, at the sympathy in the man's dark eyes. "I'd be cheating."

"Then do it different."

Do it different. A euphemistic way of saying hunt prey in the streets, use fear instead of sex. Lorcan hated it and Tomas knew it. At least with sex, his victim received something in return, even if only sexual gratification. Plus, since he preyed exclusively on call girls, he paid them well for their efforts. Lorcan shook his head slightly. "Set something up. Tomorrow."

Tomas nodded.

They both sat without speaking, staring at the fire for a few minutes.

Lorcan's thoughts returned to the original conversation. "What did the driver tell the men?"

"Nothing. He said he made an off-the-cuff remark about crazy rich people and left it at that."

"It's a reliable company, reliable employees."

"Always has been." A frown creased his brow. "I'll talk to the service tomorrow."

Lorcan nodded his approval. "Find out more about Kevin while you're at it. I want to know if someone is looking for him. His stepfather's some kind of bigwig in Washington. Walter Chambers, Chandler, something like that." A surprised gasp caused Lorcan to look up.

"Walter Chandler?"

"It means something?" The concern on Tomas' face had him worried.

"He's a senator, a rabid rightwing conservative senator." Tomas' frown deepened. "If someone found out what his stepson had been up to, there could be a major scandal!"

"You think he would do something about it?" This information did help clarify Kevin's predicament. His profession, as well as his recent means to supplement his income, would be an embarrassment to a prominent senator, especially a conservative one.

"I don't know. There's talk he plans to run for the White House in the next election. Rumor is they've started feeling out potential campaign funds."

Money. Lorcan knew his wealth gave him the ability to hide in a shrinking world but it could bring out the worst in people. "Kevin mentioned a trust fund. Find out who gets the money if something happens to him."

Suddenly the scene in the alley took on a new meaning, one, if possible, more sinister than it had seemed.

Chapter Six

The lushly appointed hotel room was cold and empty. The naked flesh of the woman standing in front of him did nothing to ignite Lorcan's desire but he had to feed. He wouldn't endanger Kevin again by going to him during a bloodlust. He had to take what he needed from this woman.

"Suck me," he whispered. The words felt hollow. Her instant obedience didn't make a difference. His flesh responded halfheartedly. Closing his eyes, he willed himself to believe Kevin's mouth sucked him, Kevin's lips surrounded his cock. With a sigh of relief, his flesh responded and began to swell. "Yes, more." His hands clenched the arms of the chair, resisting the temptation to run his fingers through her hair. It would kill the illusion to find her short hair instead of Kevin's long blond locks.

The suction deepened.

Lorcan tried to relax, get into the feeling of the hot mouth engulfing his dick. Too many things distracted him, the smell of her perfume, the slick feel of her lipstick, the unfamiliar soft groans. He had to finish this fast.

He knew he was too rough as he grabbed her hair, pulling her mouth off him. Dragging her to the bed, he pushed her down face first. Fuck her and feed. He wanted to get this over with.

Fisting his cock hard, he regained his flagging erection. His hands rough on her hips, Lorcan pulled her close and plunged into her tight passage. She wasn't ready, the lack of lubrication made her cry out. The sound of pain helped. He pulled out and thrust again. Her juices began to flow as she yelped again.

"Harder," she whimpered. "Hurt me."

Lorcan willingly complied with her request, ramming her as he slapped her ass hard. "Shut up," he growled. "You're not allowed to speak!" He slapped her again.

Her body quaked with pleasure at the rough treatment. Maybe this was the answer. Reaching to grab her hair, he yanked hard. "I want to hear your pain, not your words, bitch."

Her whimpering accompanied a fresh gush of juices. His cock now slid easily in and out of her body. She enjoyed the pain and his pleasure mounted as he manhandled her. He smacked her ass again. "You like it? You want more?"

Her head tugged against his tight grip on her hair as she nodded.

"You like my dick ramming your pussy? You want it harder?"

Again the tugging nod.

"What if I slipped it up your ass? What if I ram this," he punctuated his words with a brutal thrust, "up your ass? Would you like that?"

Her head pulled in frantic agreement at his hand. He released her hair then reached down and wet his fingers with her slick juices. One finger was soon followed by a second into her ass while slamming his cock in her now-dripping pussy.

Pushing against his fingers, she whined her pleasure. A third finger joined the first two. As he fingered her ass hard, she fisted the bedspread.

Yanking his cock out of her pussy, Lorcan guided it into her tight ass. Spasms of pleasure mixed with pain racked her body as he thrust hard and deep. He could smell her orgasm. The ripe scent was enough.

Lorcan yanked her up to his chest by her hair. His mouth fastened on her neck. Fangs extended into tender flesh. The sweet nectar of life flooded his mouth. As her body reacted to the shock with another orgasm, Lorcan's release exploded in her ass.

His bloodlust cooled with her body temperature. When Lorcan released her, her limp body fell onto the bed. Lorcan's eyes stung with shame as he checked her pulse. Satisfied with the strong, fast beat, Lorcan arranged her on the bed and covered her. Tomas would come by later and deal with her.

A stab of guilt ran through him at what he'd just done. Lorcan hadn't wanted to leave Kevin alone in the apartment. He wished he were there with his lover now.

* * * * *

Tomas was at the door when he arrived. He slipped out toward the waiting limo with a slight nod.

Lorcan appreciated the silent transition. He wasn't in the mood to talk. He wanted a shower and to check on Kevin. He had explained his absence by claiming he had a business meeting, an overseas conference call.

Kevin accepted the explanation without question, with such trust.

Lorcan hated to abuse his faith this way and hurried to his room. The stink of sex and the woman's perfume permeated his clothing. He stripped as he crossed his room to the bathroom. His discarded clothes formed a trail across the floor. He stepped into the shower stream before the water had time to warm up. The soap and water would wash the smell of the woman off his body but it did nothing for the shame. He hadn't been able to stay in the hotel room a minute longer, not even to shower.

The running water didn't mask the sound of Kevin's voice calling his name. The thought of the stinking clothes strewn across his room made Lorcan hurry and rinse. He hadn't thought about Kevin coming in here. Maybe the stench of perfume was only overwhelming to Lorcan because of his acute sense of smell.

"Just a minute," he called out as he shut off the water. After a cursory toweling, he pulled his robe over his damp body.

Lorcan opened the bathroom door to find an empty room. He was certain he had heard Kevin. His clothes were in a line toward the bathroom except for his shirt. The shirt however, was at least three feet out of place. Lorcan closed his eyes and drew a deep breath. They had to talk. Tonight.

* * * * *

The perfume from Lorcan's clothes lingered in Kevin's senses as he thought about leaving. Glancing around the room he had lived in for the past week, he stopped at the bed where he slept, and more, with

Lorcan almost since the first night. Kevin should have known he was nothing more than a plaything, a distraction for a man with more money than he knew what to do with.

Could he stay and be what Lorcan wanted? Or maybe things were different between two men. His feelings for Lorcan surprised him. Even more, if possible, than his attraction to him. All the fantasies hidden deep in his mind came to life in his lover. But they were just that. Fantasies. And maybe that's all it would ever be.

What could he do now? He had nowhere else to go. He'd given up his apartment and he didn't have enough money for another. Panic set in with the soft knock on the door. The sound of Lorcan's voice made his heart beat faster. He usually didn't ask permission to enter.

"Come in." The words came out as a whispered croak. Lorcan couldn't have heard him. He cleared his throat. "Come in," he said louder. The door opened slowly.

"Kevin." Lorcan's voice was soft but with a determined edge.

"Come in."

"We need to talk."

Kevin cringed at the words. They never boded well for him before. His mother said those words before she told him his father was dead. She also used them when she announced her marriage to Walter.

"Sit down for a minute, okay?" Lorcan's voice was soft.

Kevin nodded as Lorcan led him to a chair.

Lorcan pulled another chair over in front of his. "What I have to tell you is a little, well, farfetched. I know you aren't going to believe it at first. Then if you don't want to stay here, I'll understand. I'll set you up somewhere, help you out until you get your inheritance."

A lump formed in Kevin's throat at the thought of leaving this house, of losing his newfound lover. It was almost too much to bear. His feelings for Lorcan were stronger than he would have expected in such a short time. Not trusting his voice, he waited in silence for Lorcan to continue.

Lorcan rubbed his eyes with the heels of his hands. "I don't know where to start." With a sigh, he dropped his hands and looked at Kevin.

Kevin's heart hurt at the words. Breathing became difficult. Although barely a week had passed since Lorcan rescued him, the idea of leaving hurt.

"I wasn't looking for someone. Didn't want someone." Lorcan's eyes seemed overly bright. "My life's too complicated to include someone else in it but this has happened. I don't regret it but I have to explain the complications."

"No." Kevin shook his head emphatically. "You don't have to explain. It doesn't matter." Lorcan could have other lovers. He didn't want to lose him when he'd just found him.

Lorcan reached across the space between them and grabbed Kevin's hand. "And I want you too, I want you here. But you have to know about me, about the life I lead."

His statement sounded so ominous—the life he led. Was it crime, drugs? Was he some kind of Mafia figure shrouded in darkness? Kevin shook his head again. He didn't want to leave and nothing Lorcan said would change his mind. Kevin slid from the chair to kneel between Lorcan's thighs.

"It doesn't matter." He wrapped his arms around his dark-haired lover and murmured against Lorcan's mouth. "I don't care."

Lorcan responded with a gentle kiss.

Kevin attempted to distract him by deepening the kiss.

Lorcan pulled back. His hands stroked Kevin's face. His fingers trailed a teasing path down Kevin's neck, collarbone and shoulders until Lorcan's arms slid around him, just below his arms.

Kevin leaned into the hard body. His lips lingered on the exposed neck as he gave up his attempt to divert Lorcan. Kevin tightened his arms around him.

"But you might, when you find out. And you will find out." Lorcan's voice was a whisper in his ear. "It's why I was with someone else tonight. As much as I hated the idea, I had no choice. I will have no choice until you know the truth."

Kevin swallowed hard but refused to release his hold on Lorcan. "So tell me the truth."

"The right words are hard to find. Even after all these years, the name of my condition sounds so ludicrous to say aloud." Lorcan's arms tightened as his lips moved against Kevin's neck.

"Say it anyway."

"I'm not...exactly human."

Kevin didn't know whether to laugh or cry. What could he possibly mean? As he tried to think of a reply, Lorcan continued.

"I was once. A long time ago. But now, I'm…"

Lorcan was silent for so long, Kevin began to wonder if he should say something. What could he say? The lover who wanted to give him everything turned out to be a madman.

"Do you remember our first night together?"

Confused at the change in topic, Kevin simply nodded into Lorcan's shoulder.

"Your weakness the next day wasn't due to your injury. It was because of me. I drank too much from you, too much of your blood."

Blood? Kevin wasn't sure he heard right. His breath caught in his throat and his chest tightened.

"I have to drink at least once a week. I've always used sex as part of the feeding. Most of my kind use fear. I've never found it as fulfilling. The night we were together, I drank from your thigh. Do you remember the bruise?"

Kevin did. The spot was sore for days but it hadn't discolored much. He thought it was from the incident in the alley. When he realized Lorcan was waiting for an answer, he just nodded.

"I did that. And I want to do it again but not without your knowledge and your consent."

Kevin finally pulled back enough to see Lorcan's face. He searched the dark green eyes for amusement, humor at the tale he was telling, but he couldn't find it. "You're serious." It wasn't a question. For the first time in Lorcan's company, a chill of fear ran through him. "You drink blood? Like a vampire?"

A sad smile crossed Lorcan's lips. "As a vampire."

* * * * *

Kevin stared at the door as it closed behind Lorcan. A vampire… A vampire? "What have I gotten myself into?" A shudder ran through him that had nothing to do with the temperature in the room.

Lorcan said he had drunk his blood. Kevin rubbed the inside of his thigh where the deep ache had finally faded a few days ago. How could it be possible? Was he involved with a total lunatic? That would be the sensible answer.

And the sensible solution would be to pack his few belongings and hit the door running. But his throat caught at the idea of leaving. Lorcan stirred something buried so deep in him, Kevin hadn't realized it existed. For the first time in his life, he felt at home in his own skin. Because he finally had to admit to himself that he was gay.

"Whoa…" The idea of saying it aloud was almost as daunting as believing his lover was a vampire. Raised to believe gays were perverts, he never allowed the idea to take root.

The almost ludicrous situation struck his funny bone.

"I'm gay." Kevin chuckled. "I'm gay and my boyfriend thinks he's a vampire."

* * * * *

Lorcan woke to the sound of the opening door. From his grogginess, he could tell the sun was still high. His eyes fluttered open to see Kevin standing next to his bed.

"Kevin?"

"I thought vampires slept in coffins." Kevin's disbelief showed in his sarcastic tone and his raised eyebrow.

Lorcan couldn't stop the chuckle. "Old tales. A lot of the old tales aren't true."

"I'm staying. Though we need to talk."

Lorcan's breath caught in relief at Kevin's words. "Now really isn't a good time. I don't do so well during the day…"

Cool air rushed in as Kevin pulled the covers back and climbed into the bed. The warm body drew him close, his head rested on Kevin's chest.

"Later then."

It didn't matter if he couldn't speak. Kevin's actions said everything he needed to know.

* * * * *

The heat of Kevin's body finally roused Lorcan. Soft snores reassured him his lover still slept. Leaning on his elbow, Lorcan studied the finely chiseled features. A high forehead shadowed wide-set eyes. Long golden blond lashes any woman would be jealous of graced his eyelids. A classic nose that begged to be kissed and then his gaze stopped on the full lips. He resisted the temptation to run his fingers over Kevin's mouth. Over his lips and down to the small dimple in his chin. And then there was his throat. A long neck, the normally taut muscles relaxed in sleep. He could hear the pulse flowing through the vein in his neck, the heartbeat pushing sweet nectar through his lover.

Lorcan rolled away when the itch of his gums signaled his fangs sliding partially free. The desire to feed shouldn't be so strong. He slipped out of the bed.

Kevin stirred "Lorcan?"

"Go back to sleep." A stupid thing for Lorcan to say since they had slept all day.

"What's wrong?"

Lorcan could hear the doubt in those two words. He wondered if Kevin would always think it was something he did. All his life somebody must have told him he was wrong or bad, made him feel inferior.

"It's nothing," Lorcan sighed as he sat on the edge of the bed. He still hadn't looked at Kevin. The desire was too strong. His fangs wouldn't completely retract. He winced when the bed swayed as Kevin moved toward him. He couldn't stop a flinch when a strong hand gripped his shoulder. Lorcan closed his eyes as he clenched his fists. He had to be honest with Kevin. Nothing less would work. "I want you so much."

Lorcan gasped as Kevin's arm slid around his neck, his chest pressed against his back and soft lips moved against the nape of his neck.

"I want you too."

The confusion was so obvious. Kevin didn't understand. "I just fed. I shouldn't need to again. Not so soon. But I want you."

Kevin's grip loosened. "Oh maybe we should have that talk now."

Lorcan nodded and pulled away from Kevin. Proximity made the hunger worse. "What do you want to know?"

Kevin's snort of laughter made him turn to face him. He had moved up to the head of the bed, his knees drawn up to his chest. The tight boxer briefs outlined the curve of his tempting ass.

"Well, how's it possible?" A raised eyebrow was the only sign of his obvious skepticism.

Lorcan drew back until his back met the footboard, crossing his legs yoga style. "Where do I start?"

"The beginning." Kevin rested his chin on his knees, evidently settling in for a long story.

"The beginning... It was so long ago. My trading company, the one in the family for hundreds of years?"

Kevin nodded but didn't say anything.

"My father started it. I helped him run it when I turned seventeen. He died when I was twenty-five and I took over. I had eight younger siblings and my mother to care for." Lorcan sighed as his eyes focused on that time and place. "My mother didn't take my father's death well. She followed him a year later."

"I'm sorry... I know what it's like to lose a parent."

Lorcan shrugged. "Ancient history. Anyway, I traveled to Dublin frequently on business and for a little pleasure. Being gay in the eighteenth century wasn't easy. Every eligible female and their mother had their cap set for me. My parents never pressured me to marry and I was grateful for that. But after they died, it was like open season on me." Lorcan chuckled at the idea of running from a horde of women bent on his capture. His smile faded as he continued. "I was thirty-five when

Marius caught my attention. And he seemed interested as well. A foreigner from Romania, he said he was there on business."

Lorcan scrubbed his face with his palms. "I never did find out what his real purpose was there." Running a hand through his hair, he continued. "I preferred men from other places. I could stay detached. I couldn't very well invite a mate into my home."

"Sounds like a lonely life." Sympathy shone in Kevin's eyes.

"It was. But it couldn't be any other way." Lorcan ran his fingers through his hair. He hadn't thought of his conversion in a long time. "I'd never been with someone like him before. No awkwardness, no shame about the unnatural things we were doing to each other. It was... He bit me that first night. The pleasure coursing through me was unimaginable. I didn't even realize he did it until later. When it was too late."

Lorcan slid off the bed and stalked over to the fireplace. Tossing more wood on, he then stirred the fire with a poker. Staring at the rising flames, he began to speak again. "It lasted three days. Each night he drank until the third night, when I was so weak I couldn't move. I knew I was dying but I had no idea why. I thought I was being punished for finding so much pleasure in a man's body. When I was too weak to lift my head, he sliced open his wrist and let his blood drain into my open mouth." Lorcan stabbed the fire with the poker clenched in his hand. "I had no choice but to swallow. Almost immediately, my strength began to return." Lorcan closed his eyes and drew a deep breath. "By morning, I was like him. I hid from the daylight in his room."

Lorcan turned toward Kevin. He needed to see his reaction. "That night, I made my first kill."

"Kill?" Kevin's eyes widened and his arms tightened around his legs.

Lorcan nodded. "I eventually learned I didn't have to kill but in the early days... The thirst was terrible... I was operating on pure instinct. A hunter and his prey." He walked toward the bed.

Kevin started to move away but then stopped. "But you don't kill now? Why?"

Sitting on the edge of the bed, Lorcan continued. "I don't like killing. I never did. Now I substitute sex. That's why I was with someone else last night. I needed to feed and I couldn't take from you again without telling you the truth."

"How do you... I mean, do you have fangs?"

Lorcan laughed at Kevin's obvious disbelief. He was humoring the madman. "Yes, actually, I do. But they're hidden until I need them."

Kevin snorted. "Where? In the nightstand?"

Lorcan laughed hard at his lover's comment. "No, they're sheathed in my gums."

"Can I see?"

Lorcan's head turned to look into deep blue eyes. The strange request was one Lorcan had never heard before. Even Gustave hadn't wanted to see his fangs, had avoided looking.

The glint of amusement in Kevin's eyes confirmed his lover was still humoring him but it was a sure way to prove his story.

Nodding, Lorcan moved farther back on the bed.

Kevin moved from his post at the head of the bed and tugged at Lorcan's shoulder until he lay back on the bed.

A rush of desire, both sexual and unnatural, flooded Lorcan's body as Kevin straddled his waist. "You want to see my fangs?"

Kevin shrugged as a grin crossed his face. "If you plan to open my vein with them, I think I should."

The laugh jumped out of Lorcan so quickly he surprised himself.

A look of shock crossed Kevin's face. He must have seen what he wanted. With a slight tremble, the young man's fingers reached for Lorcan's mouth. A gentle push tickled his lip as Kevin looked closer. "You weren't kidding!" Kevin scrambled off him, falling over the edge of the bed. Jumping to his feet, he moved to the other side of the room.

Lorcan knew what he had seen. The upper right canine on both sides of Lorcan's jaw had a slight indention. The sheaths hiding his fangs were in the gums above those teeth. They opened only enough to allow the fangs to descend and were nearly invisible when retracted. Right now they were about an eighth extended, about half the length of his canines.

Sitting up on the bed, Lorcan's heart hurt at the terror on his lover's face. "I won't hurt you. I'll go elsewhere for what I need. Or you can leave, I'll find you a place."

Some of the fear faded. "I thought you were joking or cr…"

"Crazy?" Lorcan laughed. "I know. It does sound insane. But unfortunately it's true."

"Will I become like you? If I let you... You know..." Kevin wagged a finger at his neck.

"No, you have to be drained to the point of death and then drink my blood."

Kevin shuddered. "Will it kill me?"

A soft smiled played at Lorcan's lips. "No, unless I drink too much. If it hurt you, I wouldn't do it."

"Oh..." So much meaning in such a little word. Lorcan could almost hear the thoughts churning in his lover's head as curiosity replaced his fear.

"Will it hurt?"

The whispered question sent chills through Lorcan's body. "It shouldn't. It can if done to terrorize. But it shouldn't when done with love."

"Your...ah... Well, they're so small."

"They're not fully extended."

"How long are they?"

"A little more than an inch."

The curiosity in Kevin's eyes clouded with fear again.

"I don't usually extend them completely."

"Can I see them again?"

Lorcan nodded. Relief flooded through him as Kevin slowly approached.

His hand trembled as he touched Lorcan's mouth, his finger pushed his upper lip to reveal the extended fangs. "How far?" Kevin's eyes met Lorcan's. "I mean, when you..."

"Not much more than they are now. A little below the tooth."

"Show me?"

Lorcan nodded as he concentrated. Curling his upper lip enough to prevent any damage, he let the razor-sharp teeth slide free. His gaze never left his lover's face.

The fear was still there but less. Tremulous fingers cupped his cheek as an unwary thumb slid over the tip of one fang.

A small gasp escaped Lorcan's lips at the smell of fresh blood and he forced his fangs to retract.

Kevin's eyes grew wide as crimson drops formed on the pad of his thumb. He pulled his hand away to stare at the small injury. "I didn't feel a thing." Kevin's brow scrunched into a frown.

When his gaze met Lorcan's again, Kevin must have seen the hunger. How could he miss it?

With slow, deliberate movement, Kevin pressed his thumb against Lorcan's lips.

Lorcan suckled at the drops of blood. Never had an offering been so sweet, so freely given. He moaned when Kevin pulled it away. His neck arched forward to follow the sweet nectar. The sight of Kevin sucking at the tiny wound mesmerized Lorcan. His breathing became difficult as Kevin's lips met his. His cock filled hard and fast as he tasted blood in their kiss.

Pushing Lorcan down on the bed, Kevin's body melded to his—a lean, warm blanket heating his soul. Hard flesh met, pinned between them in a vise of their desire, soft, thin cotton separating them. Lorcan wanted to crawl inside Kevin's skin and take up residence there. Lorcan held Kevin tight and rolled. His lover now beneath him, he knelt to yank at the cloth separating them. His hands ran up the now-naked smooth skin beneath him, caressing each dip in Kevin's ribs, each line of muscle, teasing the aroused nipples.

"You're so…beautiful." Lorcan couldn't find another word to fit his lover.

A shy grin spread over Kevin's face. Slow hands moved up his arms until they slid around his neck. Gentle tugging brought Lorcan down into his lover's tight embrace.

Naked bodies met, legs tangled as they thrust against each other. Mouths locked, their tongues danced to an erratic tune, tangling, twisting, tasting. The slight aftertaste of blood mingled with their saliva.

His lust for Kevin's body matched the powerful desire for his blood. "Oh yes." Lorcan murmured as their sweat-slick bodies slid against each other. "You feel so good," he panted as Kevin thrust up against him.

Kevin's fingers pulled his hair with exquisite desperation as their mouths clashed, devouring each other with hunger and longing.

Lorcan couldn't get close enough to the hard body below him.

The slow cadence of their movements became faster. Soon the measured rhythm of their thrusts disintegrated as they approached climax. Their bodies grew more frantic, their cocks sliding between them, rubbing against each other with each stroke. Sweat lubricated their skin, allowing them to move more freely.

Loss of control threatened to overwhelm Lorcan. His hands slid under Kevin, grasping his shoulders, pulling them tighter. Kevin's legs wrapped around his, locking them together from shoulder to hip.

"Now," Kevin panted as he arched his head back, exposing his pale throat, offering it freely.

Lorcan's release exploded at the sheer eroticism of his lover's offer and the heat of Kevin's seed mixed with his own. Lorcan's lips fastened on the pale throat. The body beneath him shuddered as Lorcan's fangs sank into the warm flesh. Drinking the sweet liquid, his body grew refreshed as Kevin warmed his lonely soul.

* * * * *

Kevin sleepily squirmed against the warm body behind him. As he pushed into the hard muscles, the arm across his waist tightened. Soft sheets and warm blankets cocooned him and his lover.

"Hi there," Lorcan's voice murmured in his ear. "How do you feel?"

"Good..." was his lazily mumbled answer. He didn't want to move. He could spend the rest of his life wrapped in Lorcan's arms, in his bed.

"Talk to me." A breath tickled his ear before lips pressed against it.

"'Bout what?"

"How do you feel?"

Kevin had already answered him. "Why?" His eyes popped open as his hand flew to his throat. The deep ache was familiar. Kevin remembered it from his thigh but now he knew what caused it. He sat up in the bed. Too fast.

"Whoa!" His lightheadedness sent him back down onto the pillows.

Lorcan's arms cradled him. "Probably best you stay in bed for a little while." Lorcan's lips feathered across his. "Other than the head rush, how do you feel?"

"It aches. Down deep. Not the surface." Kevin's fingers kept touching the spot. His fingers feathered across two tiny bumps, like pimples on his skin. His breath caught at the meaning of those marks. "The marks are so small. I thought they'd be bigger."

"Even those will fade in a couple of hours. It has something to do with my physiology. Enzymes injected when I bite will help close a small wound. For larger ones, it doesn't help."

"Hmmm..." Kevin toyed with the almost healed flesh. Looking up into the shadowed eyes of his lover, he couldn't see the green in the darkness. "How do *you* feel?"

"Wonderful. Better than I've felt in many years." His lover leaned in to meet his lips.

Kevin welcomed his kiss. "Was it enough?" he asked as Lorcan's lips moved away.

"Yes, more than enough. I had forgotten how good it feels to be with someone I care about. For so long, I've paid to get what I need, no strings attached, no emotion. Only raw sex and sustenance."

Kevin leaned into the fingers stroking his hair. He didn't like hearing about Lorcan with anyone else but he didn't say anything.

"You've given me more tonight than all those others combined."

Kevin reached up to pull Lorcan's head down to his chest and lay in silence, listening.

"It's more than the blood and more than the sex. It's hard to explain."

"Try."

"There's an almost chemical change in human blood depending on the emotions or wellbeing of the vic—" Lorcan cut off the word.

"Victim," Kevin finished calmly, letting his fingers soothe Lorcan's crinkled brow. "Go on."

"Endorphins released in the bloodstream during orgasm are very powerful. They change the flavor of the blood as well as the element that sustains me. Some use fear. Adrenaline can have the same effect with less effort."

"Have you used fear?"

"When the circumstances required. I don't like to. I'm not as fulfilled when I do and I need to feed more often."

"And how is it different with me?"

Lorcan kept his face against Kevin's chest as he smiled at his lover's need to feel secure in their relationship. "You offered me your neck. You willingly gave me what I needed, no subterfuge, no hiding behind the sex. I didn't have to pick an inconspicuous spot, hide what I am." Lorcan rose up on his elbow to look at Kevin. "You filled all of my needs with your eyes wide open and with all of your heart. I've never had that before."

Lorcan caught the glimmer of emotion in his lover's eyes before strong hands pulled him close for a kiss. He hoped Kevin understood how much he meant to him. As much as he wanted to tell him, Lorcan held back. Gustave's loss still echoed in his heart.

Chapter Seven

A month flew by as Kevin settled on a plan for his life. Lorcan had told him he could do anything he wanted. Money wasn't an issue. Kevin didn't like the idea of being a kept man, lounging around. Boredom had already set in. His days were long with nothing to do. He decided against continuing his career in acting. Besides being a complete failure, Kevin didn't want to bring attention to Lorcan.

"Lorcan?"

"Uh-huh."

Kevin smiled at his distracted lover. Of course Kevin was responsible for Lorcan's inability to articulate. His fingers were stroking Lorcan's hard cock with teasing slowness.

"I want to finish school." Kevin finished the sentence by licking the drop of moisture on the velvet head.

"School..."

The moaned word was barely recognizable as Kevin suckled the hot tip. Kevin pulled back, releasing the heated flesh with an audible pop. "College..." He licked around the tip with long slow swipes of his tongue, pausing to concentrate on the sensitive spot below the crown.

"College..."

Kevin couldn't stifle a laugh. Lorcan hadn't managed to do more than repeat his words. His fingers rolled the tight sac of his balls.

"Yes," Kevin said before his mouth lowered on his cock again.

"Yes…" Lorcan's moan probably wasn't in answer to Kevin's idea but it was enough.

* * * * *

Kevin scheduled his classes for the afternoon so he would be able to sleep in the mornings and still be awake with Lorcan at night. His days flew by with school and studying, his nights lingered with his lover. He found he enjoyed school more than he thought he would. The first time he attended college, he was always too tired from work to actually like it, more a job than school.

And his lover offered to support his mother, get her an apartment. For that alone, he would have loved the man. Considering Lorcan's nature and their relationship, they couldn't ask her to live with them but Kevin was hopeful of a solution. The last time he talked to his mother, he was able to say he was really happy and mean it. He couldn't give her any details but she seemed relieved. Now if only he could help her. She hinted that things were better but she wouldn't listen to the suggestion of leaving her husband. His mother's situation put a damper on his happiness but he hadn't given up hope.

A soft knock at the door made him glance at the clock. Too early for Lorcan but it was time for dinner.

"Come in, Tomas," Kevin called out as he marked and closed his book.

Tomas now served him foods to help stave off anemia although Lorcan never took much. He told him the volume wasn't as important as the quality. Kevin had laughed at the image of him being like a vintage wine.

* * * * *

The soft movement in the room woke Lorcan. His senses assessed the visitor. A familiar fragrance gave him the answer.

"Good evening, Tomas."

"Good evening. Sorry to wake you early but Kevin's in the shower and I wanted a chance to talk undisturbed."

That got Lorcan's attention. Rolling out of the bed, Lorcan took an offered robe from Tomas.

"What have you found out?" Lorcan had charged Tomas to find out as much as he could about Kevin's family and background. He still wasn't completely convinced the attack in the alley was random. Something about the situation made him wary. Lorcan didn't understand why his attacker would have risked striking Kevin with a witness standing there. Unless it was the reason he was there in the first place. The rape could have been a bonus.

Tomas dropped into a chair near the table. "The trust fund is concrete. Five million Kevin can't access at all until he is thirty. No one can. Evidently, his father Marcus St. James didn't want his son to rely on the money. St. James was a self-made millionaire. If the money weren't available until much later, Kevin's father thought his son would take a career serious. His mother had more than enough money to support them and pay for Kevin's schooling. Her share of her late husband's estate was over ten million at the time of his death. Unfortunately, she gave complete control of the money to her new husband."

"Is any of it left?"

"Not much. As far as our investigator could find out, Chandler spent most of it on his senate campaigns. The way he's scrounging for money to run for the White House seems to confirm it." Tomas took a deep breath before he continued. "If something happens to Kevin, the fund reverts immediately to his mother. And more than likely she would turn it over to Chandler."

"So we have motive."

"But no proof," Tomas reminded him.

Lorcan sighed as he stared into the fire. He had taken elaborate precautions to ensure Kevin's safety. The new limo driver Donal McCann was from Lorcan's estate in Ireland. He was a trusted family member, well trained to defend himself and his charge. Lorcan purchased the limo with safety in mind, bullet-proofed and equipped with tracking technology. Kevin didn't realize Donal was tailing him at school after he dropped him off. At first Lorcan thought he was being overprotective but in light of the new information, maybe he should do more.

"There's not much more we can do without telling Kevin."

Tomas was reading his mind again. "I know," Lorcan sighed. "But he's so happy right now. I don't want anything to change that."

A soft knock on the door forestalled further discussion.

* * * * *

Reclining on the couch in the study, Lorcan read over new contracts. He paused in his work to watch his young lover as Kevin worked on the computer at the desk. Lorcan knew the depths people would go to get what they wanted. But Kevin was so young. As much as he disliked his stepfather, would the younger man believe that Chandler wanted him dead? He needed to talk to Kevin, warn him, and maybe find out more information.

His eyes focused on Kevin's flushed face. The scent of arousal wafted across the room. Lorcan assumed Kevin was studying but... "What are you looking at?"

Kevin's head jerked up and guilty eyes met Lorcan's. "Nothing."

"Okay." Lorcan shrugged. He would allow Kevin his secrets but whatever he was looking at had him hard and leaking. The scent was so strong Lorcan could almost taste him.

The nonchalant answer made Kevin blush harder.

Lorcan smiled and let his gaze drop down to the papers again. He couldn't read them. Kevin was too distracting. Ten days had passed since he last fed. He pushed a little further each time. This was the longest he had ever managed. Something about Kevin, about Lorcan's feelings for him, made it possible. At first, he thought it was Kevin's availability. No anxiety about when blood would be available, no need to be on a schedule, Kevin offered when Lorcan needed. That simple. But Gustave had been available as well.

Comparing the two men several times, Lorcan concluded the difference was their attitudes. Gustave had loved him in spite of what he was. When Lorcan took from him, Gustave grudgingly gave him what he needed only because he loved him. Kevin on the other hand, gave it freely with no qualms, no hesitation, the same as their lovemaking. Kevin took pleasure in Lorcan's pleasure. Only one thing Kevin held back on.

Lorcan remembered the panicked words in the alley when one of Kevin's attackers threatened to fuck him. Kevin's terror at the thought was too real. A finger or two was all Lorcan had managed without Kevin pulling away. Kevin obviously enjoyed it but Lorcan wouldn't push him. Lorcan was nothing if not patient. He would wait until Kevin was ready. There were many other things to do and he planned to do some of those soon.

Kevin must be ready to burst. Lorcan could almost feel the sexual tension from where he sat. Lorcan's own cock was more than willing but he resisted the urge to stroke himself, choosing to wait.

Lorcan chanced a glance at Kevin. A light sheen of sweat graced his lover's brow as their gazes met. A shiver of desire swept through him as Kevin stood and stripped off his shirt. Lorcan remained glued to the couch, watching Kevin as he rounded the corner of the desk, his fingers undoing his jeans. The predatory look in the man's eyes nearly made Lorcan come in his pants.

A string of sticky liquid formed as Kevin pulled his cock free of his boxers. Panting, he stopped in front of Lorcan, his cock swollen, glistening with moisture. Papers flew as Lorcan sat up and his mouth zeroed in on the hard flesh in front of him. Lorcan was normally the aggressor in their sex life. Kevin willingly participated but rarely instigated.

Kevin's eyes, the way he held his body screamed, "suck me", even if Kevin couldn't manage to say the words.

Lorcan was more than happy to comply with the unspoken demand.

Kevin's hips thrust involuntarily as Lorcan licked the sticky fluid from the tip of his cock. Lorcan looked up to see an apologetic look cross Kevin's features. His fingers circling the base of Kevin's cock, Lorcan used the flat of his tongue to lave the crown. His gaze stayed glued to Kevin's. "Fuck my mouth."

Lorcan's whispered words caused a shudder through Kevin's body.

Sucking Kevin in deep, he pulled on his hips. With his eyes canted up to see Kevin's reaction, Lorcan found lust blazing in the blue eyes.

Eyes that fluttered shut as Kevin moved in short, hesitant thrusts with Lorcan's urging hands. Kevin's hands came to rest on Lorcan's head and he moved faster.

Soon Lorcan released his grip, allowing his hands to rest on Kevin's hips instead of guiding. The bitter taste of come was strong as his lover's cock pushed in and out of his mouth. The strokes became deeper, faster.

"Oh God, Lorcan…"

Kevin's strangled words made Lorcan suck harder. One hand slid from Kevin's hip then around to the firm ass. Starting at the dimpled cleft, fingers slid down between Kevin's cheeks and finally to the tight hole. A slight push against the puckered flesh made Kevin come with such violence it nearly choked Lorcan. After regaining control of his gag reflex, Lorcan swallowed the hot, bitter fluid with greedy thirst.

Kevin's hands clutched his shoulders, his weight heavy. Easing the spent cock from his mouth, Lorcan caught his shaky lover and pulled him onto his lap.

"That was incredible," Lorcan whispered against Kevin's mouth.

It took a moment for Kevin's lips to respond to the languid nibbling. When he did, Lorcan thought Kevin would eat him alive. His mouth moved hungry and frantic.

Lorcan's fingers slid through his lover's long hair, pulling him away with a gentle tug. "What's wrong?"

His blue eyes were wild-eyed with fear. "I love you." The words came out as a gasp.

Lorcan wanted to reassure him with the same words but he hesitated. "Please tell me what's wrong." He thought Kevin was happy here. Whatever had upset him, Lorcan wanted to fix it.

"I want you…but I'm scared."

"I won't take any more blood." Lorcan couldn't believe Kevin was only now expressing fear.

"No!" Kevin buried his face in Lorcan's shoulder. "Not that!" The muffled sound was vehement.

Lorcan couldn't help the sigh of relief. He didn't want to think about going elsewhere for his needs. "Then what, Kevin?" Between fluttered light kisses on the bare shoulder, he whispered, "Talk to me."

"I know you want to…" A ragged breath tickled Lorcan's neck. "You always touch me there. I was looking…on the web."

Suddenly Lorcan understood. "You don't have to do anything you don't want to. Yes, I touch you. Yes, I want you in every way. But it doesn't mean we have to."

"But I want you."

"And I can wait until you are really ready, not because you want to please me."

"What if I'm never ready?"

Lorcan almost couldn't hear him, his voice was so soft. "Then we don't." His fingers ran through Kevin's hair. "Look at me," he said as he tugged at the long locks.

Kevin's eyes were bloodshot and worried.

"Can you possibly believe I have ever come away from you unsatisfied? Because if that's what you think, you're wrong. It doesn't matter."

With a slight nod, the fear in Kevin's eyes began to fade.

Lorcan pulled him close. A rapid heartbeat drummed in Kevin's chest as he cradled him. Kevin's half-dressed state reminded him of what they had been doing. His own arousal had waned as worry for his lover filled him. Now his thoughts wouldn't let go of Kevin's irrational fear. Kevin was so open about everything else in their sex life.

An ill thought crept in and wouldn't leave. "Kevin, that night in the alley. It wasn't the first time someone threatened you, was it?"

All of Kevin's muscles tensed at his words. Strong fingers dug into his arm.

"Will you tell me what happened?"

The head buried in his chest shook *no*.

"It's okay. But if you ever want to talk about it, I'm ready to listen."

Kevin nodded his head but didn't speak.

* * * * *

Itching gums woke Lorcan. He hadn't fed last night. Eleven days. Kevin had been so upset he hadn't brought it up but he couldn't go another night without sustenance. If Kevin weren't up to it, he would have to feed elsewhere. The idea of sex with someone besides Kevin was almost repugnant. He hadn't hunted for prey in years but Lorcan wouldn't pressure his lover.

A soft, familiar tread moved in the hall. Lorcan's senses grew more acute as his hunger deepened. Kevin paced the hall outside his door. The urge to go to him was strong but he decided to wait.

Kevin's silent admission last night put a different light on his worrisome lover. At first he assumed something happened as a result of his prostitution but he decided he shouldn't assume anything. As evil as people would believe him for what he was, he knew there were people out there who were worse. The soft snick of the doorknob turning let him know Kevin had made up his mind.

"Kevin?"

"Yeah."

"Come on in."

The door shut with a soft click. Kevin made his way across the dark room. The robe slipped from his shoulders as he stood next to the bed. The covers rose and the mattress dipped as Kevin joined him.

"What's up?" Lorcan asked as the warm, naked body snuggled against him.

"You didn't drink last night. It's been too long."

A swell of emotion rushed through Lorcan at Kevin's words. "You were a little distracted."

"But you need it."

Kevin moved under the covers until he was on top of Lorcan, warm thighs straddled Lorcan's hips.

Lorcan's cock began to swell as soft lips kissed his neck. His hips pushed up, seeking pressure. Hands curled into Kevin's hair as a slow rhythm developed. As much as he needed this—needed Kevin—something was wrong. A frown creased his brow as he realized Kevin wasn't responding. Lorcan ran his hands up and down the tense back. "Kevin, stop for a minute."

The lean muscles under his hands tightened even more as the kisses along his neck became frantic.

"Kevin! Stop!"

The full weight of his lover pressed down on his body in resignation. The scrape of the stubble on Kevin's cheek rubbed harshly against his neck as Kevin buried his face.

"You need blood. You said you needed it during sex."

"Oh Kevin." His arms tightened around the limp body on top of him. Lorcan rolled them until they were on their sides facing each other. "Yes, I get more of what I need during sex but only if you get pleasure too. Something's bothering you. You don't have to force it."

"I don't want you going to someone else."

"I won't. If I have to, I'll hunt instead. I'm a little weak right now but not in dire need." Lorcan hated lying. He was more than a little weak and he would require blood soon — tonight.

"No! It's too dangerous for you to hunt. You could be found out."

"So talk to me. Let's get past what's worrying you."

"I can't." Kevin's eyes closed over the pain.

"I won't make you. I'll never force you." Lorcan settled into the pillows and pulled Kevin close. His lips traced across the frowning forehead.

"Drink anyway. If hunting helps, if it doesn't have to involve sex, drink now." Kevin's eyes opened and met his. "It would work, wouldn't it?"

Lorcan hadn't thought of it. Of course, without the added kick of adrenaline or endorphins, he might need to feed sooner than normal. By then Kevin's mood might be lighter. "Yeah, I guess." A soft laugh punctuated his surprise at Kevin's suggestion. "I never tried it that way."

Kevin arched his neck, offering his throat.

Lorcan thought he had never seen anything so beautiful. His fangs began to extend at the sight.

Kevin's hand slipped around his neck and pulled him down toward the tempting flesh.

"Drink."

His lips mouthed the tender skin sheltering the warm life-giving liquid before sucking with gentle pressure. A soft moan reminded him of the sensitivity of his lover's neck. He laved the area with the flat of his tongue. The salty taste mixed with the memory of Kevin's cologne.

"Do you have any idea how much you mean to me?" Lorcan whispered in his ear. The tip of his tongue traced its way back down to the fine blue line under his skin. The slight stubble teased his tongue.

A sweet-sounding gasp caused his fangs to extend farther. His fingers feathered across Kevin's chest, discovering a hardening nipple. His fingers tweaked the tiny nubbin of flesh. The body beneath him arched against the pressure. Lorcan suckled at the spot he needed. Razor-sharp teeth penetrated the layers of skin, tender flesh, seeking the warm, rich liquid. A rush of fluid hit his tongue, revitalizing his weakened muscles almost immediately. Slowly, with exquisite care, he drank, not taking as much as he needed but enough to last for a few days.

Sated for now, his fangs retracted. He licked the tiny wounds, gathering the last minute traces of blood from the skin. Lorcan's hand drifted down and found Kevin hard.

His lover moaned as Lorcan grasped him and began stroking. Lorcan kissed him hard as Kevin's hips arched, pushing his cock through the hand holding him.

Kevin's arms grabbed for Lorcan's head, holding him tight as their mouths locked. His hips convulsed with frantic movement as his tongue fought to gain control of Lorcan's. "Oh yes…" Kevin gasped as warm, sticky seed flowed over Lorcan's hand.

Lorcan milked him with long, slow strokes until his lover finally relaxed. Their kisses gentled, becoming lazy nips and soft nibbles.

Lorcan grinned at his sated lover. "I've never used that particular brand of biting as foreplay but it seemed to work." He planted a gentle kiss on his forehead. "I'll be right back." Lorcan rolled out of bed, switching on the bedside lamp before he walked away.

Blinking at the sudden brightness, Kevin's gaze followed his lover as Lorcan walked toward the bathroom. The lean muscles rippled with his every move. Lorcan had given him so much. He wanted to be able to give Lorcan everything he needed, everything he wanted. Sated and feeling a little lethargic from blood loss, he lifted his hand to his neck. His fingers gingerly touched the tiny marks. It still amazed him the bite didn't hurt.

Lorcan had explained it once. His fangs injected an enzyme to deaden the nerves and help close the wounds. Only a slight ache, deep where the tissue was forced apart, was left.

Lorcan cared for him, gave pleasure and security. He wouldn't hurt him. Not like— His thought broke off as Lorcan kneeled on the bed.

A warm wet cloth in hand, his lover cleaned his stomach and his now-flaccid cock with gentle, efficient care. Kevin noticed the semihard state of Lorcan's erection.

"You haven't come yet." Kevin wished he could have managed more than a whisper. "Make love to me."

"I thought that's what I just did." Lorcan laughed, tossing the washcloth on the nightstand before he slid under the covers next to Kevin.

"No, I mean..." Kevin took a deep breath and exhaled a long slow breath. "I want you in me."

"Why now?" Lorcan's tone was startled.

"You wouldn't hurt me." Another deep breath. "You... It... He hurt me. But you wouldn't."

"Never."

"Please."

A shiver ran through Lorcan's body. "Are you sure?" he whispered against Kevin's lips.

"Yes," Kevin said, relieved his voice sounded confident.

"If you change your mind, say so. I'll stop, no questions, no problem. I'll stop."

Kevin nodded his agreement but he wouldn't stop him. The bed dipped and rose as Lorcan moved away. The sound of the drawer opening next to the bed sent a shudder through him. They had used lube before but knowing what Lorcan would use it for tonight caused him to breathe a little faster.

"We don't have to do this."

Kevin smiled at his lover's voice. He didn't miss much. "I know. I want to."

And he did. Kevin wanted this so much. He knew it could feel good. When Lorcan's fingers teased him, it felt wonderful. Last night, looking at pictures on the web, he had been so turned on he had practically attacked his lover. But the memory of what happened before...

His dark thoughts fled as Lorcan's fingers fanned across his chest. Warm breath tickled his ear.

"You don't have to prove your love. This can wait until you're sure." His leaking cock told a story different from the reluctant tone. The idea alone had restored Lorcan's arousal.

Kevin smiled into the shadowed eyes watching him. "I want you." Kevin rolled onto his side to face him. "I want this," his fingers encircled the weeping hard flesh, "inside me."

Lorcan's body jerked at his touch. "Oh yes." The words slurred into a moan as Kevin stroked him.

Strong arms tightened around him, holding him close. Kevin's spent cock twitched with interest at his lover's reaction. Suddenly, the thought of Lorcan fucking him didn't seem so daunting. He loved him more than he thought possible. If it made Lorcan happy, made the man practically melt with pleasure at the idea, Kevin could, would, do it.

"Stop…" Lorcan pleaded. "I won't make it very far if you keep that up."

Kevin released him with a bit of reluctance.

Lorcan's hand moved from Kevin's back, sliding down to caress his ass. It lingered, feathering strokes on his ass for a brief moment before it moved down to his thigh. Long fingers tugged at Kevin's leg until it draped over Lorcan's hip. Running back up his leg, those gentle fingers teased up and down the crack of his ass before disappearing behind him.

A snap of the cap on the lube made Kevin's heart race. A slick finger returned and made its way down to the sensitive pucker.

Kevin couldn't stop the shudder racing through his body. It didn't deter Lorcan. They had done this before. Lorcan loved to tease him, prod his prostate until Kevin's very soul shook with pleasure.

The tip of a cautious finger worked its way into the tight channel. Lorcan kept Kevin's lips occupied with a slow kiss as his finger made slow, lazy circles to relax the tight ring of muscle. As the invading digit pushed deeper, Kevin tightened his leg around Lorcan's hips.

"Relax, Kevin," Lorcan whispered against his mouth. "It's easier if you relax."

Kevin nodded and forced his calf to fall limp against Lorcan's ass. Soon Kevin was pushing against the rhythm of Lorcan's finger and his cock reawakened from the exquisite stimulation.

A second finger pushed in beside the first. Kevin groaned against Lorcan's chest.

"Yes... More..." Kevin had never taken more than two fingers before he pulled away but tonight he wouldn't stop his lover.

Lorcan's body jerked at his words. His fingers slid free.

"Don't stop," Kevin moaned.

"Just for a second."

The snap of the lube made him relax against the warm light fur of his lover's chest. He couldn't help the reactive clench as Lorcan slathered the cold gel on his hole. Three well-lubed fingers pushed slowly inside. The stretch burned but it wasn't painful. Kevin's dick ached and he wanted more. He wanted Lorcan.

"Fuck me." Kevin pushed against the fingers filling him as he spoke. "Please." He pushed again. "I want you."

"Oh yes." Lorcan breathed. His fingers slid from Kevin's body. "Roll over on your stomach. It's easier."

"No!" The loud sound shocked even Kevin. "No," he said softer. "I need to see you."

"Okay." Lorcan nodded. "Okay." Understanding colored his tone as his hand urged Kevin onto his back. He grabbed several pillows and pushed them under Kevin's hips. "We'll do it this way."

Kevin breathed a sigh of relief. He surprised himself with the vehemence of his response. His lover just smiled as he kneeled between his legs. The loving look in Lorcan's eyes reassured him. A swell of emotion nearly overwhelmed him. A man, he had fallen in love with a man. He had never allowed himself to admit to his attraction to men, never considered sex with a man until the circumstances of his life got out of control. The blowjobs he'd given for money never aroused him, never did anything but disgust him.

But the man framed by his thighs, preparing his cock to invade Kevin's body, provoked desire a woman never had.

Some of his feelings must have shown in his face. Lorcan paused as he stroked his cock with lube. Leaning over him, his kiss was tender, loving, and silently said everything Kevin needed to hear.

"I want you," Kevin whispered against the firm lips. He grinned at the groan his words caused.

Moving back up, Lorcan's lube-coated fingers once again slid into Kevin, slicking the tight passage, pressing the lube deep. Kevin moaned as Lorcan teased his prostate. And then the fingers were gone. Lorcan pulled Kevin's legs up against his chest, his heels resting on Lorcan's shoulders. The blunt tip of his lover's staff sought entrance to his body.

Panic insisted on rearing its head. Kevin clutched at the bedding, forcing his eyes to focus on the man in front of him. Lorcan…not a nameless stranger in an alley, not someone intent on punishing him. Lorcan…making love, not forcing him.

"We can stop." Lorcan kept his hips held perfectly still in spite of his rapid breathing.

"No." Kevin took a deep breath. He pushed against his lover's erection to emphasize his words. The burning sensation made him gasp but it didn't really hurt. Twinges of fear more than pain caused his hard-on to wilt. But this wasn't about him. "More…" His fingers were numb from holding the sheets so tight.

Lorcan pressed forward a fraction of an inch at a time. Kevin could see the struggle on his face as he maintained the slow pace. A fine sheen of sweat lined his face and chest.

Kevin's tongue circled his dry lips at the idea of licking the moisture from his lover's skin.

"Breathe, Kevin. Relax and breathe." Lorcan's hands rubbed his stomach, his thighs.

Releasing a deep breath, Kevin gave in to the urge to push. His breath caught in a gasp as his lover filled him. Lorcan's balls, soft and hard at the same time, pressed against his ass. The burn was intense as was the feeling of fullness, but the whimper from Lorcan had to be the sexiest sound in the world.

"Oh Kevin…" Lorcan sighed before leaning forward, intense eyes boring into Kevin's. "Are you okay?" His gaze sought the truth.

"Yes." Kevin had trouble getting words out. "Good." He moved his legs until they encircled Lorcan's waist. The slight movement seated his lover even deeper.

"You feel wonderful. So tight... So good..." Lorcan whispered as he leaned forward to kiss him.

Kevin arched up, chasing Lorcan's lips as he straightened. A gentle, short stroke sent Kevin back into the pillows.

Lorcan pulled one leg up against his chest, kissing Kevin's calf as he moved. The pressure against his prostate renewed Kevin's arousal. Soon Lorcan's strokes lengthened, though still slow and gentle. His gaze never left Kevin's face.

"Yes. Faster..."

Lorcan changed angles, his strokes moving upward, nailing his prostate each time.

"Oh yes." Kevin reached for his cock, now aching with the unfamiliar stimulation. He didn't miss the flare of desire in Lorcan's eyes as he pulled at his cock with hard, rough strokes. "Harder."

The strain in his body was obvious. Lorcan wouldn't last much longer. Green eyes kept flitting between Kevin's eyes and his hand.

Wicked thoughts of how to tease his lover ran through his mind. His hand matched Lorcan's rhythm. "Lorcan, yes— Faster." Soon the hard cock pounded his ass.

Lorcan's hands tightened on his legs hard enough to bruise but Kevin didn't care. Tremors shook his body as his balls tightened. Thick white come shot hard enough to land on Kevin's face and neck. His ass muscles spasmed around Lorcan's cock. Scalding heat filled him as Lorcan's body stiffened.

Cries of ecstasy mingled as Lorcan emptied himself with short jabs of his hips. He leaned over Kevin until his body pressed heavy and he took his mouth in a hard kiss.

Between mouth-bruising kisses, frantic whispered words finally coalesced into something recognizable. Kevin's heart soared at the words.

"I love you. I love you."

Chapter Eight

୫୨

Lorcan sensed Tomas' soft measured footsteps before they stopped outside the bedroom door. It was early but he was already awake. A willing supply of blood made rising slightly before sunset less difficult. Kevin's presence in the apartment made him more than willing to rise early. Lorcan grinned at his thoughts. Kevin made him rise quite often these days.

After the first time Kevin allowed him to make love completely, his young lover had become almost wanton. Lorcan was grateful for his unnatural stamina. As a mere mortal, he might have trouble keeping up.

"Come in, Tomas. Stop lurking." Lorcan swung out of the bed and grabbed his robe.

"I didn't want to disturb you," Tomas said as he walked in. "I needed to talk to you before you see Kevin tonight. You will have to talk to him soon."

"What's wrong?" Three months had passed since Kevin moved in. Nothing unusual had happened so far. He actually considered giving in to Kevin's requests to ride the subway to school.

"I think Kevin knows Donal's following him."

"Why?" Lorcan couldn't understand how. Donal was very good at what he did.

"Twice today, Kevin's given him the slip. Donal found him both times but today he's sure Kevin saw him. You need to tell him the truth. Otherwise, he could end up in danger without anyone to back him up."

Lorcan responded with a soft sigh as he watched Tomas stoke the coals from last night's fire. "Do you think he is in danger?" he asked as Tomas turned back toward him. "We never found any evidence of foul play. Did I overreact?"

"I've thought about it. We might be taking unnecessary precautions. But if we were right and didn't do something about…" Tomas' voice trailed off to let Lorcan make his own ominous conclusions.

Lorcan scrubbed at his face with his hands. "I hate to scare him. He's so happy. His whole bearing and attitude is night and day from when we first met."

"I know." Tomas sighed.

Lorcan knew Tomas understood. The older man had become very fond of Kevin. Tomas had never married and had no children. In spite of their appearances, Lorcan was more of a father to Tomas. Kevin managed to fill an empty spot in Tomas' heart. Lorcan regretted the life the older man was required to lead but he needed someone he could trust.

"I'll talk to him. But I'd like to talk to Donal first."

"I thought you would. He's waiting in the study."

* * * * *

When Lorcan entered the room, Donal stood.

"Sit…sit…" He waved at Donal. Lorcan worried about what the man had to say. A few times Donal had suspected someone of following Kevin. He dutifully reported it to Tomas and Lorcan. Each time the person had been someone different. As long as a pattern didn't develop, Lorcan refused to worry. "What makes you think Kevin knows you're following him?"

"Twice now he's changed his routine, left a class by a different route. If he were choosing a shorter route to where he was going, his choice wouldn't have bothered me. Both times, the route ended up being a longer way to his next class. Today he was late."

"Are you sure he's not being followed by anyone else?" Lorcan noticed the slight hesitation before the other man spoke as if Donal chose his words carefully.

"I can't say no. I know the few times someone appeared to be following him turned out to be a false alarm. It's just... One of those made me very...uncomfortable."

"How so?"

Donal fidgeted in his chair. "The way the guy looked at Kevin." His gaze shifted between Lorcan and his hands several times.

"You can say anything you want, Donal. You don't have to be delicate. Just say it." Lorcan's voice encouraged him softly.

"The guy looked as if he really had it bad for Kevin. I'd swear he was sporting a hard-on just watching him."

"What?" Lorcan couldn't help the sharp tone. This was news to him. Donal hadn't mentioned it before.

A worried frown wrinkling his brow, Donal stood. "Sir, I never saw the guy on campus again, and I made sure to not let Kevin out of my sight after that. I think it's how Kevin caught me. I was tailing too close."

"I'll talk to him. Tonight."

"So you want me to continue the surveillance?"

Donal's posture was stiff, almost at attention. "We'll see, Donal. I need to hear what Kevin has to say about the situation."

* * * * *

Kevin was sure Donal had been following him at school. He didn't know what he'd done to make Lorcan mistrust him. In a way, it pissed Kevin off but he didn't say anything to Lorcan. Insecurity still taunted him in spite of Lorcan's constant words of love. Instead, Kevin managed to lose Donal a couple of times to see Donal's reaction. The man had been frantic.

Kevin was sure Lorcan wasn't a cruel man but Donal's fear had been real. Did Donal tell Lorcan what happened? Would he be punished? What would Lorcan do if he knew Kevin was aware of the situation?

The fire burned low but Kevin didn't move to stir it. The weather was warm enough to do without a fire but it gave Kevin a sense of security His life had been a dismal failure until he met his lover. For the first time in his life he loved someone he thought loved him back. The idea of confronting Lorcan about Donal was daunting. He really didn't want to find out he wasn't trusted, didn't want it confirmed.

"Hi there." Lorcan's words startled him.

"Hi." A lump in his throat formed at the sight of his lover. Kevin didn't know what else to say.

Lorcan settled into the chair opposite Kevin and joined him in staring at the glowing embers. Tension filled the silence.

"I have a confession to make."

Kevin's eyes darted toward the sound of the words. He swallowed hard, thinking about what it could mean.

"I know you found out about Donal following you."

Kevin nodded. What could he say?

With a heavy sigh, Lorcan stood. Pacing the floor in front of the fire, he ran a hand through his unruly curls.

Kevin waited, silent at first as his lover wrestled to find the words, but he was afraid of what Lorcan would finally say. "I don't know what I've done wrong, Lorcan, what I've done to make you mistrust me."

"Oh God, no, Kevin!" Lorcan knelt in front of him. His hands caressed Kevin's face. "You haven't done anything wrong! I don't want you to leave!"

"I thought… You had Donal watching me. I assumed—"

Lorcan's lips stopped his words. Small gentle kisses covered his mouth before Lorcan pulled him into a tight embrace.

"I had him watching you because I thought you needed protection."

"Protection?" That was the last thing Kevin expected to hear. "Why?"

Lorcan released him, pulling away to look into Kevin's eyes. "I… The whole incident in the alley just struck me wrong. The man who hit you could have killed you. Why would he risk doing that with a witness? After you told me about your family, your trust fund, I had Tomas hire an investigator."

"You checked me out?" The part about someone trying to kill him paled in comparison to the idea of

Lorcan looking into his background. Some things Kevin didn't want Lorcan to know about. Not yet.

"I checked out your family, Kevin. I wanted to know if someone had a reason to hurt you. I can't stand the thought of losing you."

The emotion glistening in Lorcan's eyes convinced Kevin the truth of his words. "And what did you find out?"

"Your stepfather would benefit the most from your death. He needs money. If something happened to you, your trust would go to your mother and—"

"And she'd give it to him."

"Yes."

Walter hated him, but would he have him killed? Kevin was an embarrassment to the man, always had been. His career, his attitude, hell, even his hair length, managed to piss off Walter. Did he hate him enough to take such a risk? Walter wanted the White House. Would he risk an investigation into Kevin's death? Would he risk someone uncovering his part in it? Of course, he knew things that could ruin Walter's chances of ever holding elected office again. Would he risk the death of his stepson to keep Kevin silent? "Did you find any proof?"

"No." Lorcan whispered the word against Kevin's lips.

"So you had Donal watching." Donal's frantic search for Kevin made sense now.

"Yes, but evidently he wasn't doing it too well. You saw him."

"Only twice. If he's been following me for almost two months, I guess he's not too bad."

"Yes, but now what do we do? Do you think your stepfather would try to hurt you?"

Kevin sighed as he leaned into Lorcan's arms. His face sought its customary spot in Lorcan's neck. "I don't know. He's not what he appears to the public. Walter's a cruel man when it suits him."

"You know this for sure? Something he'd want you dead over?"

"Yes." Kevin really didn't want to talk about it, ever. But maybe Lorcan needed to know. As reluctant as Kevin was to relive the past, maybe it was time he dealt with it.

Lorcan gazed into the troubled blue eyes. "You can tell me anything, you know."

Kevin nodded against him. "Hold me."

Happy to comply, Lorcan's arms tightened around Kevin.

"He used to beat me." Kevin's voice was soft, a little slurred against Lorcan's neck, as if the words fought to stay in.

Lorcan suspected as much. From what he'd learned about Walter Chandler, the man would have insisted Kevin be obedient and conform to his will.

"He was always mad. Most of the time I didn't even know why."

Lorcan's hands rubbed soothing circles on his lover's back and kept quiet.

"It started almost as soon as he and Mother were married. At first she tried to protect me. He would get mad at her for interfering. It was easier to take what he did than to watch him hurt her."

Lorcan's anger welled up. His blood boiled at the idea of the man hurting an innocent child.

"I tried to do what he wanted, how he wanted it, so he wouldn't start hitting." Kevin's voice was tight with emotion. "It wasn't so bad there for a few years. I did whatever was expected of me, behaved the way he wanted." A shudder racked Kevin's body.

"I've got you," Lorcan whispered.

Fingers tightened on Lorcan's arm, fingernails digging deep.

"He...uh...caught me when I was...fifteen." Kevin's voice shook with remembered fear. "I was jerking off." The words rushed out. "He had explained sex to me. Told me it was forbidden... Only perverts masturbated." A ragged gasp tore from him. "He said if I wanted to be a perv, as he put it, he'd show me what that word really meant."

Lorcan didn't need to hear the rest but if Kevin said it aloud, maybe it would help him heal.

"He hurt me." Kevin's tense body shuddered, his face buried in Lorcan's chest.

"He can't hurt you now." Lorcan wondered if anyone had held the injured child he had been, had comforted him.

"It only happened once. He sent me away to boarding school afterward. Told me it never happened and if I told anyone, he would find out." His breath caught, almost a sob. "I never said anything until now." The last words came out as an exhausted whisper.

"It's okay. He'll never know." Lorcan wasn't certain Kevin heard his soft words of reassurance.

Rocking Kevin slowly as if he were still the abused child from years ago, Lorcan decided he would keep Donal watching, whether Kevin wanted it or not. If Chandler was serious about running for president, the man he raped as a teenager would be a major liability.

* * * * *

"If Donal's going to be following me, I'd rather he be with me instead." Kevin knew he was losing the argument over Donal's surveillance so he proposed a compromise.

"What do you mean?"

"Have Donal enroll to audit the rest of my classes this semester. He won't have to follow me. No one will try anything if he's there. I'll be safe without having to look over my shoulder for him all the time."

His lover was silent. Lorcan at least seemed to be giving the proposal serious consideration.

Kevin felt foolish having a bodyguard tailing him. The more he thought about it, the more he couldn't believe Walter would do anything now. If his stepfather thought he would be outed, he would have done something a long time ago. Walter's senate races couldn't have handled the scandal any more than a presidential one. What difference would it make now? Five million dollars wasn't near enough for a presidential campaign. That amount couldn't possibly help enough for Walter to risk harming him.

"Okay." The word was almost grudging. "We'll try it your way."

Kevin snorted, refusing to look apologetic. His way would be allowing him to go alone. He knew it wasn't going to happen.

His lover glared at the rude noise. "Kevin, try to understand. I can't let anything happen to you. I don't care if the possibility is remote, as long as there is a possibility, I will protect you."

Kevin sighed and nodded his head. He agreed for Lorcan's sake. Strangely enough, telling Lorcan about Walter last night took a weight off him. Maybe confession *was* good for the soul. A weight lifted from his chest. For the first time since the day his mother introduced them, Kevin felt free from Walter's influence.

Chapter Nine

ಣ

Since Donal had always been in the front of the limo, Kevin hadn't gotten to know him so Kevin was surprised to find him a good companion. A dry sense of humor and a ready joke made Kevin laugh more than he had in a long time.

When Donal expressed a real interest in college, Lorcan agreed to let him enroll for real in the fall. He wouldn't get credit for auditing the classes this semester with Kevin but he could take them for credit in the summer.

Taking the summer off while Donal retook the classes meant Kevin could keep Lorcan's schedule without worrying about school during the day. As soon as he made it through finals, Kevin would be free to spend more time with him.

Lorcan's idea of more time was intriguing to say the least. Lorcan had several homes in Europe and they were spending the summer traveling between them.

Kevin hadn't been to Europe since his father died. When Walter and his mother traveled, they always left him at home with sitters or at boarding school. The anticipation made Kevin antsy. He found studying difficult with the excitement of travel looming.

Of course, he knew Lorcan thought he was safer out of the country. Kevin could indulge his paranoid lover.

After all, it gained him a tour of Europe with Lorcan at his side.

When the door opened behind him, Kevin ducked his head back to his books.

Tomas had become quite the taskmaster over his studies. In many ways, Tomas had replaced the father Kevin barely had time to know. He watched out for him, talked about his day, kept him fed and took care of him.

All of a sudden, Kevin had a family again. Even Donal, only a few years older than Kevin, he'd come to regard as a brother.

"Time for dinner," Tomas announced.

Kevin had finally convinced the older man they should eat together instead of serving him in his room. Donal joined them and mealtimes became fun instead of just necessary.

"Coming," Kevin said as he shut his books. He wasn't getting a lot done today anyway.

*****

The sound of laughter greeted Lorcan as it drifted down the hall from the dining room. His household had changed so much since Kevin moved in. His young lover banished the loneliness, not only for Lorcan but also for Tomas. He wished he could stay up during the day to share in their lives. At night, his life became all about Kevin. Before Kevin came, Tomas kept the same schedule as Lorcan. With Kevin's arrival and enrollment in school, Lorcan insisted Tomas take care of the younger man. He missed his time with Tomas.

Happy with their plans for the summer and no need to lead separate lives, Lorcan was anxious for Kevin's finals to be finished. They were scheduled to leave after Kevin's last test next week.

Lorcan worried about Kevin's passport though. They had applied for it almost two months ago. Tomas had checked on it several times in the last few weeks. There was no reason for it not to be issued but the office of Homeland Security held it up. No one seemed to know why. Lorcan hadn't told Kevin yet.

Gut instinct told him Kevin's stepfather had somehow delayed the issuance but Lorcan had no proof. Chandler wouldn't get to Kevin in Europe. Since the senator was on the committee on Homeland Security, he would have the power and the contacts to hold up a passport. More than likely the relationship between Chandler and Kevin would have shown up somewhere. Lorcan was more than a little nervous. They had used Lorcan's address on the application. If Chandler managed to find where Kevin lived, Lorcan was afraid he would be in more danger now than before.

Not for the first time, he wished he had taken a different route. He could have excellent forgeries made without too much trouble. He had decided against it for Kevin's sake. The younger man was gaining the confidence someone his age should have. Lorcan was afraid to ask him to give up his identity when Kevin was only now figuring out who he was.

Forcing a smile before he entered the dining room, Lorcan kept his concerns to himself. He didn't want to spoil their fun, not yet.

* * * * *

Kevin and Donal walked across campus toward the parking lot. Fortunately, Kevin convinced Lorcan to get rid of the limo in favor of a black Lexus. Kevin always felt conspicuous in the limo. Although Kevin was perfectly capable of driving, Lorcan insisted Donal drive. As the only condition to the change in cars, Kevin agreed. He still wasn't sure all the precautions were necessary. Since Donal turned out to be a friend more than a bodyguard, Kevin let it go.

Kevin had one last final and he was done for the semester. "I wish Lorcan would let me go to finals alone. You must be bored sitting and waiting for me."

Donal laughed. "Not a chance in hell. And you should stop pushing it."

"Do you really think there's someone out to hurt me? You've been following me all semester. Have you seen anything to make you believe it?" Kevin glanced at his friend.

"Not really. Nothing concrete." The man's words were hesitant.

There was something but Donal wouldn't admit to it. "So what exactly did you see? Lorcan treats me as if I'm fragile and sometimes I feel that way but this is my life and my safety. I should know what's going on. I won't say anything."

Donal nodded a slow agreement as they approached the Lexus. "Wait 'til we get in the car, okay?"

Kevin agreed and hurried his steps. For weeks he had pestered Donal for information and he was in a hurry to find out what was going on.

As soon as they settled in the car, Kevin turned to his friend. "So what is it?"

Donal backed out of the parking spot before saying anything. "A couple of times I thought someone was following you. One of them had me worried."

"Worried? How? What did he do?"

"It was more how he looked. How he looked at you."

"Looked at me?"

"Almost hungry, sexual. It's hard to describe. I just had a bad feeling about him."

"Have you seen him again?" A sick knot formed in the pit of Kevin's stomach. What if one of the men he had serviced recognized him? What if it was one of his would-be rapists?

"No, but I'm not sure he didn't see me. If he realized you had someone watching you, he might back off until he had a chance at you alone. So you're never alone."

Kevin leaned back his head and closed his eyes. He didn't want to remember the humiliation of what he'd done. He hadn't paid attention to the faces of the men he'd sucked. Having their cocks haunt him was enough without their faces branded in his memory as well. He never thought about them remembering him, looking for him.

The things Lorcan taught him made Kevin realize he hadn't done a very good job on his knees. Of course, most men didn't care about finesse as long as a hot mouth was willing.

"You know about me, don't you? About what I was doing when Lorcan found me."

Donal's face was impassive. "Yes."

Kevin knew Lorcan would have told him. Donal needed to know to protect him but hearing it confirmed made Kevin sick to his stomach.

"It doesn't matter, Kevin. Sometimes people end up in situations where they do things they regret." He grinned at him. "Stupid things, granted. I don't judge you. I've been lucky. Lorcan's looked out for the members of my family all my life and for years before. My grandfather was his manservant long before I was born. Tomas took over the role when my grandfather died. I've never had to worry about making a living. I always knew I'd work for Lorcan. I don't look at you any differently."

A lump of emotion formed in Kevin's throat as a strong hand grasped his shoulder.

Donal's gaze met his as they stopped for a red light. "I'll help him keep you safe. But you have to help me do it."

Kevin's hand covered Donal's as he nodded his agreement.

* * * * *

Tomas waited at the door when they arrived home. A frown lined his normally passive face.

"What's wrong?" Kevin asked as he set down his books on the table in the foyer.

"Your passport has been denied."

"What?" Kevin and Donal spoke the word in unison.

"Kevin, is there anything you could have done to account for it?" Tomas' voice wasn't accusing, just confused.

All their plans for Europe flew out the window. The news hit him like a sucker punch. Queasiness settled in the pit of his stomach. "Not that I know of. I've never done anything except for, well, you know. And I never got arrested for it or anything."

Suddenly all of Lorcan's suspicions about his stepfather hit home. Walter had to be behind this. Who else could have done it?

"We'll talk to Lorcan when he wakes." Tomas shook his head. "I'm not sure what to do next or if we want to do anything at all."

"Not do anything?" Kevin wanted this trip and he thought Lorcan and Tomas did too.

"It's not always safe to bring too much attention to Lorcan and his affairs. We don't welcome scrutiny."

Well, it made sense. Lorcan wasn't exactly in a position to have people checking out his background.

"Yeah," Kevin said with a nervous laugh. "I understand."

"Take your books and go study. We'll talk to Lorcan when he wakes." Tomas shooed him off.

Kevin grabbed his things from the table and headed to the study. He could hear the low voices of Tomas and Donal as he walked down the hall but couldn't make out what they were saying.

He tossed his books on the desk and dropped into the chair. His mind wouldn't focus on American history right now and he knew it. Unease crept up his back at the thought of Walter interfering in their lives. Things had been so wonderful these last few months. He was almost able to forget Walter existed. To have him intrude now sent a mix of emotions through Kevin. Anger battled with fear, disappointment jumped into the fray. Kevin only wanted to live his life. Why couldn't the world and Walter Chandler stay out of it?

* * * * *

Lorcan knew Kevin was upset. He hadn't said more than two words all evening. Normally he regaled Lorcan with stories of school or things he had done during the day with Tomas and Donal. His lover had been so excited about going to Europe.

Lorcan had homes in London, Paris and Vienna, as well as the family manor in Ireland. They planned to visit all four places. Now their plans were tangled in red tape.

Lorcan didn't know where to go from here. He had a contact at the British consulate. He was a member of the family but one who didn't know about Lorcan's special situation. He hesitated contacting him. Maybe Tomas could, or someone from back home. Maybe he should have Tomas arrange for a passport through their contacts, at least as a backup. Lorcan would feel much better with Kevin as far away from Walter Chandler as possible. He'd talk to Tomas later.

Lorcan had converted a spare bedroom to a gym for Kevin. Standing in the doorway watching his lover beat the hell out of a punching bag, Lorcan sighed. As much as he enjoyed the view of Kevin's back rippling with each blow, they needed to hash this out. "Talk to me, Kevin."

"What about?" Kevin's tone was noticeably angry. "About the fact," he slammed his fist into the bag, "Walter is still trying to run my life?" Covered in only a pair of shorts and sweat, Kevin turned to face him.

"About the fact I'm a prisoner in this house. I can't even go for a walk without Donal shadowing me!"

His heated words startled Lorcan. Guilt swept through him. "I didn't know you felt like a prisoner. I didn't mean for you to. I'm sorry."

"Oh damn! No, Lorcan." Kevin took a deep breath. "I'm sorry. I just… I was looking forward to getting out, doing something, without having to look over my shoulder all the time." Kevin's face changed from anger to remorse in seconds. As he moved across the room, he yanked off the boxing gloves. "I'm sorry. I didn't mean it like that." He caressed Lorcan's face with a sweaty hand.

Lorcan tasted salt as he kissed his lover's palm. "No, don't apologize. I realize you've been restricted in your movements and I'm sorry about it. I want you safe." Lorcan hadn't thought about how the restrictions affected Kevin. He should have known playing hermit would be difficult on the young man.

"I love you for it, for taking care of me. Not to mention, I'd probably be dead if you hadn't come along."

Lorcan pulled him tight against him. "The idea of not having you with me…" The lump in his throat forced his voice to a whisper. "I have to keep you safe. Promise me you'll help by not—"

"I know. I won't do anything stupid. I just wish there were some way to make Walter leave me alone. I know it has to be him. Who else?"

"I don't know," Lorcan sighed. "Is there any other reason, anything you could have done, something, no matter how insignificant, to keep you from getting a passport?"

Kevin shook his head as he leaned against Lorcan. "No, I've never been in trouble with the law or anything. Never been involved in any kind of subversive group or activity. There shouldn't be anything on my record other than my relationship to Walter."

"I'll see what I can find out but I have to make discreet inquiries. I can't draw too much attention to myself."

"I don't want you to do anything to endanger yourself," Kevin said, his tone tight. "It doesn't matter. We don't have to go anywhere."

"But we will one day need to move. I can't stay in one place too long. Although I keep to myself, people start to wonder why I don't age. I've already been in New York for ten years. Ten years of looking thirty-five. In a few more, people will notice."

"I hadn't thought about it."

Lorcan kissed Kevin's frowning brow. "There are a lot of things I have to consider. Don't worry about it. Even if we can't leave now, things could change in the future. Or we move someplace else in the States."

"Do you have other homes here?"

"No, but I have plenty of money. Nothing to stop us from buying somewhere else."

The frown slowly smoothed off Kevin's brow. They stood holding each other lost in thought.

* * * * *

Kevin tossed his books on the table in the foyer as he and Donal walked in the door. "Tomas, we're home! And I think I aced the history exam!"

In spite of their aborted travel plans, Kevin was elated to be free for the summer. More time to spend with Lorcan regardless of where they spent it.

"In the living room, Kevin, Donal," Lorcan's voice called out.

The two men looked at each other, eyes wide in surprise. Still full daylight, Lorcan was up hours earlier than he should be. They turned into the room to find three men waiting with Tomas and Lorcan.

"What's up?" Kevin asked. The three men were in suits and looked too official for Kevin's taste. A glance at Lorcan showed him to be pale from the effects of daylight.

"These gentlemen are with the Secret Service. Seems your stepfather will be announcing his candidacy for president soon." Lorcan's voice shook with exhaustion.

"I'm Special Agent Roger Malloy." The man flashed a badge at Kevin and Donal. "This is Agent Downey and Agent Leland. As a member of Senator Chandler's family, we need to assess your situation."

"My situation is just fine. Is this the reason my passport was denied?"

"It wasn't denied, it was delayed," Malloy said in a gruff tone with a glance at Lorcan. "Mr. MacKenna expressed his concern in that regard."

"You've screwed his plans for the summer. I think it would concern him and me as well."

"It can be fixed but we need to be sure of your safety. The Secret Service has to ensure all members of the candidate's family have adequate protection."

"And I'm so sure my stepfather is concerned for my welfare. We haven't spoken in three years. I would prefer to keep it that way. I don't intend to help him into the White House and you can bank on me never being on his campaign trail. So release the hold on my passport and let me get on with my life." Kevin didn't miss the look of amusement on Lorcan's strained face. Finally, Kevin had a target for all his frustration.

"Mr. St. James, we, and I include you, have no choice. You could be a pawn to force the senator into situations we would have to deal with."

"I am safe here. I would be safe in Europe with Lorcan. You don't have to worry about me or spend taxpayers' money where it's not wanted. Now if you'll excuse me, Lorcan is ill and doesn't need the excitement. Please process my passport immediately. And don't bother to give my stepfather my regards." Kevin marched over to his lover and took his hand to help him from the chair. With his arm wrapped around Lorcan's waist, Kevin guided him out of the living room.

"You shouldn't have gotten up," Kevin admonished his lover as they walked toward Lorcan's room.

"They asked to see me. I had no choice. Besides, I wanted to know what was going on."

Lorcan stumbled as they entered the bedroom. Kevin half carried him the rest of the way to the bed. He pulled the tie on Lorcan's robe then slid it off his shoulders.

"Get in bed."

With slow painful movements, Lorcan complied.

It hurt Kevin to see him so weak but he knew how to fix it. Stripping off his shirt, he climbed into the wide bed with his exhausted lover.

"Drink," he ordered as he leaned over Lorcan, his neck bare.

A week had passed since Lorcan last fed. The added strain of rising during daylight hours would have weakened him. Fortunately Lorcan didn't argue. Soon the familiar gentle sucking teased Kevin's throat as Lorcan took what he needed.

* * * * *

Kevin slipped from the bed after Lorcan fell asleep. He worried about the scrutiny this would cause. Already it had endangered Lorcan, forcing him to rise during the day. Kevin wouldn't let anything happen to his lover, even if he had to leave. As much as the idea hurt him, as much as it would hurt Lorcan, it might be the only answer.

Lorcan couldn't handle people watching him. Reporters, rivals for the White House, there were so many things to worry about with Walter's candidacy a reality. If they could have gotten out of the country before it happened, the situation wouldn't be so bad. Now he wasn't sure what he should do.

Voices drifted toward Kevin from the living room. They wouldn't still be here, would they? Almost an hour had passed since Kevin left them but there were too many voices to be Tomas and Donal. On silent feet, he approached the door to eavesdrop.

"I'm sorry, Mr. O'Dwyer, but it's not that simple. We have to watch him whether he wants it or not. He could be at risk."

Sounded like Malloy.

"You heard him. He and his stepfather aren't even on speaking terms," Tomas replied.

"It doesn't matter. We need to speak with him again. Please get him."

"I will not disturb Mr. MacKenna again. Kevin won't leave him until he's sure he's all right. If you want to wait, then fine, otherwise please leave." Tomas' voice strained with tension.

"I'm here," Kevin said as he moved to the doorway.

"Mr. MacKenna?" Tomas' expression mirrored Kevin's worries.

"He's resting. I gave him something to drink and he went back to sleep." Kevin tugged a little self-consciously at his shirt collar.

Tomas understood and some of the tension left the older man's body.

Kevin turned to Malloy. "I will not allow you to disturb Mr. MacKenna again. I will not allow you to invade his privacy. I don't want, nor do I need, your protection. I want nothing to do with Walter Chandler or his bid for the presidency. You can tell him for me if he doesn't call off the watchdogs, I will make him regret it. I want my passport here within the week. If it isn't, then maybe I'll do a little announcing of my own. And he won't like what I have to say."

Malloy's brow wrinkled into a frown. "Do you have some information we should be aware of?"

"I could make up stuff and the press will eat it up. Walter has made me miserable since the day he met my mother. I would be happy to return the favor. Now if you will excuse me, I have things to do." Kevin motioned toward the door. "Please leave."

The three men shuffled toward the door, obviously unhappy with the interview. Malloy turned for one last attempt. "Mr. St. James, this affects your mother as well as your stepfather. You should think of her."

The man's words made Kevin even more angry. How dare he try to use his mother against him? "I have thought of her. Every day since I left her there with that monster. But she won't leave him. Now get out."

The startled look on the faces of the three agents was genuine. They must have no idea of the poor relationship between Kevin and Walter.

"Does he know you're here?" Kevin asked quickly.

"I don't know. I haven't spoken with him personally. It's standard procedure though. He should know we would contact all members of his family."

"Well, don't consider me a member of his family. I don't. Good day."

Kevin stalked out of the living room toward his bedroom. Seeking the safety of his room, he let his body react. Falling into a chair, Kevin shook with shock. Everything was crumbling around him. If he didn't get his passport, if they insisted on watching the house, Lorcan would have to leave without him. No place in the States would be safe from the Secret Service. If Walter actually won the presidential race, Kevin wasn't sure there would be any place in the world they would be free of him. Anger welled up in him. Nearly six months of happiness with Lorcan. Was it all he was allowed?

*****

As soon as his eyes snapped open, Lorcan rolled out of the bed. His nap combined with the unexpected gift of blood renewed him. Grabbing his robe, he didn't bother to dress before seeking Kevin. He wished he hadn't been so weak earlier. If he fed more often, it wouldn't have bothered him but he dared take only so much from Kevin.

His young lover was sleeping, still dressed, his body curled into a tight ball on his bed, a pillow hugged tight to his chest.

Lorcan slid onto the bed, pulling Kevin close. Kevin fought him for a moment in his sleep but relaxed as his eyes opened.

"Lorcan, are you okay?"

"I'm fine, thanks to you."

Kevin snorted as he pulled away. "No thanks to me. You wouldn't be in this situation if it weren't for me."

Lorcan wanted to keep Kevin in his arms but he released his hold. "Kevin, it's not your fault."

Kevin didn't seem to hear him as he paced the floor. "You have to leave without me. You can't be here if they are watching the apartment. You should go on to Europe as planned."

Lorcan sat up, shaking his head. "I'm not going anywhere without you. Don't even bother."

"Then I'll leave. I won't endanger you!" Kevin shouted. "You don't understand! If something happened to you, I couldn't live with it. I couldn't live knowing I had caused your—"

"You won't! I can protect myself. I've been doing it for over two hundred years!" Lorcan's tone matched Kevin's as he stalked over to him. Grabbing him, holding him tight, Lorcan continued in a softer tone. "I'm not leaving you, ever. Do you understand? Separating is not an option. I can't live without you." He emphasized his words with a harsh kiss.

Kevin responded in kind with rough hunger. Lorcan manhandled him back to the bed, pushing him down on it, his body covering him. Lorcan needed him too much to consider leaving him behind.

Their bodies pushed and pulled against each other, frantic in their need. Lorcan found himself on bottom when Kevin rolled them over.

His lover's hands were rough as they yanked his robe open. Kevin's mouth and fingers were everywhere at once, kissing, licking and pinching his way down Lorcan's body. His cock swelled fast as Kevin's hands yanked his boxers down with rough need. A hot mouth teased his balls as Kevin's hand stroked his hard flesh.

Lorcan pulled the bedding loose as his hands fisted the material. Kevin was rarely aggressive in their lovemaking and it drove Lorcan wild when he was.

His lover's tongue moved up his cock, licking up to the top. Gentle lips sucked at the sweet spot below the head before his tongue circled the tip. One hand tightened around the base as the hot mouth swallowed him.

Lorcan couldn't stop the cry of joy or the bucking of his hips. Kevin took him deeper, encouraged his thrusting. Just when Lorcan thought he could take no more, the amazing heat left him.

His eyes opened to see his beautiful lover standing near the bed, stripping, hands shaking with desire. Lorcan's cock ached for his lover's body. Kevin opened the drawer of the nightstand, reaching for the lube.

"I want you," Kevin whispered between kisses planted the length of his body. His weight rested on Lorcan, their cocks lined up together. "Fuck me."

Lorcan couldn't stop the urge to thrust up against the hard body covering him. "Yes. Oh God, yes." He rolled them over until Kevin was pinned under him. Bruising kisses, hard thrusts against each other, and Lorcan was already on the edge of climax.

"Now. Please..." Kevin's voice was tight with desire.

Lorcan grabbed pillows from the head of the bed and stuffed them under Kevin's hips. His hand shook as Kevin opened the lube and squeezed some into Lorcan's palm. His fingers slid down to the tiny puckered hole. His cock ached to take him, fill him, but Lorcan reminded himself of the need to be gentle as he slid one finger into his lover to prepare him.

"No, fuck me." Kevin moaned. "Now—fill me up with your cock."

Lorcan grabbed his shaft tight, pulling at his balls to keep from coming right then. They had always made sure Kevin was well prepared before penetration. Lorcan never wanted the memory of pain to be part of their lovemaking. "Love, it would hurt."

"No, it won't. It's not like it's the first time. Just fuck me, please."

Kevin was right. They had done this many times before. Lorcan could see the flare of desire in Kevin's eyes as his hand moved to his cock. The lube was cold and helped calm his overheated flesh. Barely maintaining control, Lorcan pressed the tip against the tight ring of muscle guarding his lover's hot passage.

Kevin had never been this tight before. He was ready to pull away, prepare Kevin properly, when the muscle loosened and his aching cock pushed past the barrier.

Kevin breathed deep and relaxed his body.

Lorcan's hard flesh slid home, balls-deep in his lover. "So tight," Lorcan moaned. "So incredible…" The last words a mere whimper.

Leaning forward to kiss Kevin, he felt strong legs encircle his waist.

Kevin wrapped his arms around him as he moved with tiny strokes.

"Too good. I won't last."

"Then don't," Kevin whispered. "Fill me up."

Lorcan buried his face in Kevin's neck. The scent of his blood pulsing so close to the surface, Kevin's hard cock pressed into Lorcan's stomach. His need for this man overwhelmed him as Kevin met his thrusts, his tight ass contracting around Lorcan's dick.

"Come for me." Kevin's harsh whisper breathed against his ear. "Drink." The delectable throat rubbed against his mouth. "Feed on me, fill my ass. I want you so much."

Lorcan's body reacted to the words. His release filled his lover's tight hole as his fangs sank into the offered vein. The sticky heat of Kevin's seed smeared his stomach. So lost in ecstasy, several seconds passed before he remembered he had already fed earlier today. His fangs retracted in shock.

"Kevin!" He looked at his lover to see pale features, a wan smile. "Oh damn, what have I done?"

Kevin smiled. "What I asked you to..." His eyes closed into sleep.

* * * * *

Kevin's arms and legs felt tied to the bed. The weakness extended to his head as well. His neck didn't want to work properly. He could hear soft voices in the room.

"I don't know what happened. I lost control!" Lorcan berated himself for Kevin's physical state.

"He'll be okay, Lorcan. He hasn't lost as much blood as he did the first time. His color's coming back already. He'll be weak for a couple of days, that's all." Tomas' voice reassured Kevin but he didn't think Lorcan was buying it.

Kevin knew he would have to leave and soon, before Walter's announcement was official and the full scrutiny of the world descended on him. The idea of living without Lorcan scared him much more than dying. He almost wished Lorcan had taken every drop. To die in his lover's arms, their bodies intimately joined, would have been a blessing. No more worry, no thought of living without his gentle dark lover. But the guilt Lorcan would suffer would be unbearable. Kevin knew the trusting offer of his neck was a powerful temptation to his lover. He shouldn't have done it.

Besides he didn't really want to die.

"I'm all right. Stop talking about me as if I weren't here." Kevin winced at the weakness in his voice.

"Kevin." It took mere seconds for Lorcan to arrive at his side. "I'm so sorry, love. I shouldn't."

"Don't say it. I wanted it. I wanted you."

Light from the hallway followed by the sound of the door closing let Kevin know Tomas had left.

"But I know better. I could have killed you."

"But what a way to go." Kevin regretted the words as soon as they left his mouth.

A flare of pain and anger lit Lorcan's eyes. "If you ever try that again, I'll feed elsewhere. I'm not risking you."

"I won't. I promise." Kevin knew his lover was serious and the idea of Lorcan feeding from someone else wasn't a pleasant one. But he would have to eventually. Kevin had to leave.

"Why?" The anger in Lorcan's eyes faded to confusion.

"I needed you. Needed to have you in every way I could. I'm going to lose you. We can't stay here together and we can't leave. But one of us has to go." He was pleased his voice didn't shake. His stomach was another story. He didn't know if the blood loss made his insides jump or if it was the idea of losing Lorcan.

"No." Lorcan shook his head. "Not going to happen."

"Don't you see? If we stay here together, you could be in danger. I won't let my life destroy yours." He had to make Lorcan see reason.

"I'm not leaving you." Lorcan's face was grim. "I don't care."

Kevin swallowed hard and looked away. "Then I'll leave you."

"So tonight was goodbye? Is that what you were doing?" The anger was back.

Kevin hadn't thought about it but maybe Lorcan was right. He was saying goodbye. One way or another, they would have to go their separate ways. "Maybe."

"No. I won't let it happen."

"Lorcan, please! Hear me out."

His lover's flinty stare didn't change.

"You go to Europe, take Tomas. I'll stay here at the apartment with Donal. I'll be safe here. This place is a fortress. You can see to your homes and maybe they'll issue my passport in the meantime. I could join you then." Kevin doubted he would ever see his passport but if it got Lorcan out of harm's way, he would try it.

"I'm not leaving you."

"Then you can't stop me from leaving. And anywhere else I won't be safe." Kevin was playing dirty but he had to get Lorcan out of New York, away from the scrutiny of the outside world. "Think about it, okay?"

Lorcan's nod was reluctant.

Kevin was too tired to argue anymore. "Hold me," Kevin whispered. He breathed a sigh of relief as his lover slid into the bed beside him. He would miss Lorcan desperately but Walter had left him no choice.

* * * * *

Lorcan worried about Kevin. He'd recovered from his overindulgence of a few days ago but Kevin was melancholy and depressed. Lorcan couldn't stand the thought of leaving him but the fear of Kevin doing something stupid made him consider it.

If Kevin stayed here, he would have a degree of protection even without Lorcan. Kevin was right about the apartment.

Built like a fortress because Lorcan designed it that way. Of course, he had designed it over fifty years ago. The walls were thick and the doors solid. Trouble with another vampire at the time made the reinforced home a necessity. Fortunately the workers didn't question the eccentric rich man. Especially when they were well paid.

The walls served their purpose then. With his people safe in the reinforced apartment, Lorcan was able to deal decidedly with the rogue creature stalking him.

Ten years ago when he moved to New York, he had a state-of-the-art security system installed. If Donal stayed here with Kevin and Lorcan sent over another trusted servant, his lover should be safe without him. But Kevin wouldn't be close. Lorcan didn't know if he could stand it.

Another option existed but Lorcan hadn't mentioned it yet. He would talk to Kevin tonight.

His step conveyed a confidence he didn't feel as he headed to Kevin's room. He didn't want anything to change but if it had to, he wanted to stay as close to Kevin as possible. Knocking lightly, Lorcan entered without waiting for a response. "Hi there." His voice was soft.

His morose lover glanced up. Kevin's eyes were dry but bloodshot. He didn't know whether from crying or lack of sleep. Either way, Lorcan needed to make it better.

"Hi." The one word held so much pain.

Lorcan moved close, pulling him into a rough hug. "It will be okay. I'll make sure it is."

"You can't. Once again, Walter has my life in his hands, finding ways to hurt me. He won't let me go. Maybe he does want me dead."

"I have a proposal. It could relieve your fears and mine."

A brief glimmer of hope flickered in Kevin's eyes but it faded all too fast. "The only answer is for you to leave."

"No, I was thinking you could leave but to another apartment. One nearby but not too close."

"Leave here?"

"Yes, I'll set you and Donal up in an apartment, one with security. You would be safe and I could visit you."

"But it would be dangerous for you to be seen with me."

Lorcan kissed any further protest from his lips. "Remember what I am. I can move without being seen." Lorcan hadn't discussed the differences his immortal state gave him. Kevin never asked. His inhuman speed, strength and senses would make his visits to Kevin nearly impossible to detect by others.

Kevin's arms tightened on his neck.

"We can still see each other." Lorcan rubbed slow circles on his back, holding him tight.

"I didn't want you to go." Kevin's sigh of relief was hot against Lorcan's neck. "I couldn't stand the thought of not seeing you again."

"It won't come to that. I already have Tomas looking for a place. Donal will be with you so you won't be alone."

"I'll miss you anyway. Not being able to see you every day."

"Me too. But it's better than not seeing you at all." He pulled up Kevin's chin so he could look in his eyes. "So this will satisfy you? As far as my safety goes?"

Kevin nodded then leaned his face into Lorcan's hand. "Yes. I think it'll work."

Chapter Ten

Kevin couldn't get accustomed to the new apartment. The bed was too hard and the room too bright. The wide windows allowed too much sunlight. He smiled at the idea of his lover living here. The windows alone made Lorcan shudder.

Tomas had assured them both of the security of the building even as he ordered heavy curtains and blinds for the windows.

The worst part was the loneliness. Lorcan made him vow not to leave the apartment without Donal. Unfortunately his friend was in class. A nap to prepare for Lorcan's weekly visit tonight would kill a couple of hours. He missed his lover's hard muscles against him, his cock invading his body. Still fearful of Lorcan's safety, Kevin only agreed to see him once a week because of Lorcan's need for blood. He was relieved Lorcan wouldn't need to seek out someone else.

Rolling over to look at the clock, Kevin sighed then closed his eyes. Only four in the afternoon, four more hours before full dark, until Lorcan's visit. More caged here than he had been at Lorcan's, Kevin punched the pillow in frustration. At least there, Tomas kept him company. He wanted his life to be in his control. Not Walter's, not even Lorcan's. He'd chosen to leave. Actually, he issued an ultimatum to Lorcan. Since he made this choice, he should feel in control.

The phone interrupted his thoughts. Relieved at an excuse to get up, he rolled out of bed to answer it. "Hello?"

"Kevin…"

The hesitant voice on the other end brought painful memories flooding through him. "Walter, how'd you get this number?"

"So it is you. How do you think? I have connections. Haven't you figured it out yet?"

Kevin could picture Walter's self-satisfied smirk.

"Yeah, I figured it out. If you don't leave me alone, I'll make you pay. You know I can ruin you. I would have preferred to forget your tender instructions but I can bring it out now. You'll never get in the White House. You won't even regain your seat in the Senate when I'm through with you." Kevin surprised himself with the confidence in his words.

"No one would believe you. I've told everyone about my poor, misguided stepson. How you hate me because I wasn't your father, although I tried. How you refused my help when you went to New York, ended up whoring yourself on the street. You'll see it all leaked to the media over the next few weeks. You saying anything will simply look like a case of sour grapes."

"I don't think so. Even the hint of scandal has brought down politicians before. You'll fall, regardless of what lies you've told." Kevin hoped his voice didn't reflect the rising nervousness.

Walter could do a lot of harm. He might be right. People might not believe him without proof. Kevin wished he could have recorded this conversation.

"Well, it won't touch me because you won't say a word to anyone."

"And how do you think you're going to stop me?"

"Because if you do, your *friend* Donal may not make it home from school one day."

Kevin cringed at the threat. The emphasis on the word friend told him Walter thought Donal was his lover. Physically, he did resemble his ancestor. After all, Donal was descended from Lorcan's brother and the coloring and the build bred true.

"Donal is trained to take care of himself. You'd better rethink your threat."

"Well trained against a car accident? Or a subway one? So many dangerous things are found in New York."

"Release my passport and we'll leave the country. You'll never hear from me again."

"What, and let you try to ruin me from a country I have no power in? I can't let that happen, son."

"Don't call me son," Kevin growled through gritted teeth.

"Remember what I said. Your little boyfriend is good at keeping you out of trouble, but he's not so careful when he's by himself." Walter's chuckle caused shivers down Kevin's spine. "Take care. Son." The last word sounded dirty.

As the phone line went dead, Kevin couldn't catch his breath. Walter would keep him here, keep him quiet and if he got out of line, he'd kill Donal. Together shame and relief washed over him. Walter had no idea his lover was Lorcan. Of course Donal had shown up at Lorcan's close to the same time he did. Now they had moved into an apartment together. It would make sense to Walter.

Kevin had to warn Donal. He dialed Donal's cell phone and waited impatiently for the answer. Donal was supposed to keep his phone on and available to Kevin at all times. Kevin bit his lip in frustration as the ring rolled to voice mail.

"Donal, it's Kevin. Watch your back. Call me as soon as you get this message. But whatever you do, watch your back!"

He glanced at the clock as he hung up the phone. Ten to five, at least three hours until he could talk to Lorcan. Donal's last class would be ending any time now.

* * * * *

Frantic with worry when the door finally opened, Kevin was about to call Tomas. He even considered talking to the Secret Service men who perpetually parked outside the apartment building.

"Where the hell have you been?" Kevin didn't think. He just yelled.

The surprise on Donal's face was almost comical. Almost.

"I called you nearly two hours ago!"

"Calm down, Kevin. My phone is missing. I must have dropped it. Then I had a flat tire when I got to the garage."

Kevin's body shook from relief combined with fear, relief Donal was here, safe. Fear… Kevin doubted Donal dropped his phone or one of the new tires on the Lexus would have gone flat on its own. Walter was demonstrating his power. Nothing would convince him different. His adrenaline rush flat-lined. He would have fallen if Donal hadn't caught him.

"Kevin, what's wrong? What happened?" Donal helped him to the couch.

The concern in his friend's eyes forced him to calm down. He had to tell Donal what happened but first, Kevin had to find his breath.

* * * * *

Rage filled his heart and mind as Lorcan paced the floor of the new apartment. Senator Chandler would learn to leave them alone. His first urge was to drain the man of his last drop of blood. Not only had he threatened Kevin, now he was threatening Donal as well. He would find a way to stop the senator, to ruin him, to make him pay for the agony he'd caused Kevin.

Kevin sat silent, watching him. A tinge of fear lined on his pale face. Kevin had never seen him in a killing rage.

It didn't help that Lorcan hadn't fed in a week. For Kevin's sake, he had to calm down. He couldn't approach his lover like this. He might cause inadvertent harm.

"I'm sorry, love," Lorcan softened his words. "I'm upset but not at you." He sat across from Kevin and took a deep breath, releasing the storm of fury as he exhaled. "I don't like it when people close to me are threatened."

The look of fear on Kevin's face eased. "I don't either," Kevin sighed. "I don't know what else to do. He's not going to leave me alone. This won't end until I'm dead."

"No!" Lorcan's mind flashed with fear. "You are not the cause. You won't be the solution."

"You were right from the beginning. I would have died in that alley. The cops would have written it off as another hooker killed in action. My stepfather already started his story about me, about what I was doing. He would have looked like the grieving father, probably won votes for it. I'm a danger to his chance at the White House. He won't leave me alone until one of us is dead."

The rage evaporated, replaced by the tender feelings Lorcan had for his lover. Moving close to Kevin, his arm slipped around Kevin's shoulders. "Had he treated you differently as a child, you probably would have become the man he wanted you to be. If he had loved you like a father should, you'd be beside him on the campaign trail. It's his fault. Not yours. But it led you to me. It allowed me to love you. I promise I won't let anything happen to you or Donal."

Lorcan breathed a little easier as Kevin leaned into him.

"I want him to leave us alone."

"I know," Lorcan sighed as Kevin's face burrowed into his neck. "Me too." Lorcan made a silent vow to make it happen. He wasn't sure how.

* * * * *

Kevin snuggled his back closer against Lorcan. He hadn't been much in the mood for sex but he welcomed the nearness of his lover. His mind wouldn't stop thinking about Walter. Talk about a turn-off. The clock showed nearly one. A few more hours until Lorcan would have to leave. The worst part of living separately was waking alone. He wanted their life back.

"You're thinking too hard," Lorcan's voice whispered.

Kevin should have known he wasn't sleeping, after all the night was his day but Lorcan insisted Kevin rest. After the initial adrenaline rush faded, he felt as weak as if Lorcan had drunk too much so his objections hadn't been too strenuous. "I can't stop. It's driving me crazy. No matter which way I turn, he's there."

"Come here." Lorcan pulled at his shoulder.

Kevin turned over to face him. His eyes were almost black in the dim light.

"We'll figure something out. I need a little time. I'm bringing over several people from the London office and one from Paris. You and Donal will be safe." Lorcan's hand brushed back Kevin's hair. "I want them to continue thinking you and Donal are together. It gives me room to move around and ask questions. Donal is my cousin. Well, kind of. At least on paper. I can ask questions about him. I don't have to mention you."

"Donal and I have already talked about it. As long as no one knows about you, you're safe. We prefer to keep it that way."

Lorcan's arms tightened around him. The scrape of slight stubble on his neck reminded him Lorcan hadn't fed. It had been a week though it seemed much longer. Living apart made the days drag and the nights worse. Lorcan couldn't chance showing up every night. Now Kevin was wasting precious time feeling sorry for himself.

He tightened his arm around Lorcan. One hand found his lover's dark curly hair. Pulling his mouth tighter against his neck, he whispered, "Taste me."

It didn't take long for Kevin to feel the now-familiar sucking and the slight dizziness from Lorcan's feeding.

Lorcan drank with deliberate slowness, drawing out his pleasure. Kevin never failed to amaze him. Several times now feeding had become part of their foreplay. The lack of sexually laced endorphins didn't seem to diminish the affects of the blood on Lorcan's metabolism. Kevin's willingness to give him what he needed seem to enhance his blood in a way sex never could.

Kevin's fingers relaxed in Lorcan's hair.

After licking the tiny wounds to ensure closure, he kissed his way up Kevin's throat to find his mouth. "What you do to me…" Lorcan whispered against the full lips.

"Look what you do to me," Kevin countered. His hand tugged at Lorcan's until it covered his hard erection.

"Why does my bite affect you this way?" Lorcan lazily stroked the heated flesh as he spoke. "I've never had a lover like you before."

"I don't know. I guess I've never had anyone need me before. Want me, yes, but not need me. You need me."

"I do but not just for the blood. You know that, don't you?"

"I know." Kevin's blue eyes shone bright in the dim light. "Make love to me. I want you inside me."

Lorcan smiled. He grew excited when Kevin voiced his wants and needs. Usually his boldness came out when Lorcan fed or when Kevin was feeling vulnerable. He wasn't sure which caused the attitude tonight but few things Lorcan could deny his lover. What he was asking for now was definitely not one of them.

Kevin's hand slid under the pillow searching for something.

Lorcan couldn't help but grin when his lover held up the lube. Lorcan accepted the offering. Keeping their mouths connected with deep, drawn-out kisses, he moved to hover over Kevin, his weight on his forearms. He savored the taste of his lover as their cocks lined up between their bodies, fitting together as if made for this.

Long drawn-out kisses made Kevin growl with pleasure. The sounds of his lover's moans were music to Lorcan's heart. Lorcan missed his daily presence so much it was physically painful.

Parting from Kevin's lips with a mixture of reluctance and anticipation, Lorcan began a slow exploration down his lover's body. Pausing at the first stop, his neck, he licked and kissed each sensitive spot he could find. Pausing at the tiny, precious wounds, Lorcan circled each with the tip of his tongue. A soft whimper made him smile. He bathed the area in gentle kisses before moving down to the spot slightly above his collarbone. Again the soft, barely audible groans let him know he was making the most of the journey.

Kevin's hand moved to Lorcan's head, fingers tightening in his hair. "Oh yes." Kevin's panted as Lorcan moved on from his neck.

The next stop paused at Kevin's nipple, Lorcan's tongue teasing the tiny nubbin of flesh. His hand moved to stroke the straining erection.

Kevin's hips jerked upward at his touch. The fingers in Lorcan's hair tightened to the point of pain made exquisite by his lover's desire.

Lorcan switched to the other nipple. "Can't play favorites," he whispered before he gave it equal wet, loving treatment. The vocal accompaniment of his lover's cries made his cock ache for Kevin's tight ass but Lorcan wasn't rushing this. They had so little time together, he wanted to enjoy each moment.

Kevin's hips moved in time to his strokes and his moans kept rhythm.

Lorcan's tongue teased its way down the tight abdomen to the soft hair below the navel. Sticky fluid already leaked from his lover's cock. With a few nipping kisses down Kevin's lower stomach, Lorcan reached his goal. Panted moans followed as Lorcan licked the moist tip of his lover's erection. Kevin's hips arched as Lorcan's tongue swirled around the velvet head.

"Yes…" Kevin slurred the word as Lorcan's mouth finally engulfed his cock. Throaty panted words punctuated Lorcan's strokes. "Oh God, yes! Suck me. Please. Yes!"

Lorcan quickly lubed his fingers before his mouth descended on Kevin's cock. Slick fingers zeroed in on the puckered goal. The first touch caused Kevin to arch up into Lorcan's mouth. He took him all, following Kevin's hips back down as his finger slid into the silky passage. By now, Lorcan knew exactly where to apply pressure. A second finger followed the first and it didn't take long.

The varied sighs, pants and moans from his lover were an erotic symphony.

"Oh yes! Lorcan! I'm coming... Coming..."

Bitter fluid gushed across Lorcan's tongue as his lover gave up his essence to the hungry mouth. Drinking from his lover's cock as eagerly as he drank from his veins, Lorcan milked him dry.

Hands fisted into the bedding now relaxed in the afterglow of orgasm.

Moving slowly, not wanting to disturb his lover's bliss, Lorcan settled between Kevin's thighs.

Kevin's eyes followed his movements, filled with love and exhausted ecstasy while Lorcan prepared his leaking cock.

With slow, deliberate pressure, he pushed into the tight velvet heat. Once again, Kevin's voice rose with pleasure, serenading him with sounds of desire.

"Yes. Fuck me..."

Kevin's legs wrapped around Lorcan's waist and arms rose to pull him down. Their lips met in slow, languid kisses matching the strokes into Kevin's body.

"More... Faster..."

As Lorcan complied with his lover's demands, their kisses became more intense, deeper, hungrier. Muffled cries swallowed by each other's mouths escalated. Kevin's arms and legs tightened on Lorcan's body as his hot seed erupted, filling the younger man.

* * * * *

Lorcan didn't want to wake Kevin. He hated saying goodbye, leaving him like this. To have found so much with him only to have their life interrupted by Walter Chandler's machinations was devastating. Kevin couldn't hide his disappointment when Lorcan left but leaving without waking him wouldn't make the situation easier.

"Wake up, sleepyhead." Gentle strokes on Kevin's back finally roused him.

"Mmmm... Come back to bed." Kevin's eyes hadn't opened yet.

"Can't, love. I have to go."

Eyelids flew open, blue eyes filled with realization. "What time is it?"

"About an hour before dawn."

Kevin nodded. "You need to go." Although his words were firm, his eyes betrayed his sadness.

"I love you."

"And I love you."

Lorcan knew he couldn't stay. A strong desire to throw caution to the wind and curl up beside Kevin threatened. Instead he leaned over and brushed a tender kiss across Kevin's lips. "I'll talk to you tonight."

Kevin nodded again. "Okay."

As Lorcan closed the door on his lover's bedroom, he resolved once again to find a way to fix this.

Chapter Eleven

ଇଠ

A black mood engulfed Kevin and nothing he did would relieve it. His finger hooked the heavy curtain and pulled it aside to stare out at the world. Anger welled up at the sight of the black car. It sat in front of the apartment building day and night. The suits in the car never got too close but Kevin still resented the Secret Service's presence. Nearly a month had passed since he and Donal moved.

Walter hadn't called again but Kevin was ready with recording equipment if he did. Kevin was tempted to contact Walter himself but it would make the man suspicious. He wouldn't get him to say anything incriminating.

Sheer boredom wasn't helping.

Donal was cramming a full semester's prerequisites into one summer so he could enroll in the same classes with Kevin in the fall. He wasn't around much during the day. At night, Donal buried his nose in his books.

No amount of computer games, television or working out could stave off Kevin's cabin fever. His blood boiled at the thought of Walter's interference. The anger was futile. Kevin couldn't do anything about it and the helplessness made it more painful.

Worrying about it didn't help anything. It made Kevin more depressed. He plopped down in the recliner near the window and picked up his book. Instead of the mystery novel distracting him, his mind kept wandering back to his predicament. The sound of the telephone was a welcomed distraction. "Hello."

"Mr. St. James?"

The voice on the other end wasn't familiar. "Who's calling?"

"There's been an accident. Mr. McCann has been injured."

Donal injured? "Oh my God! Where is he? Is he okay? What happened?" As they tumbled from his lips, the questions ran together.

"He's unconscious but stable. He's been hit by a car. We've also contacted," Kevin could hear the rustling of paper in the background, "Tomas O'Dwyer. He's on the way to the hospital."

"Which hospital?"

"The NYU Medical Center."

"I'll be there as soon as I can!" Kevin hung up the phone and ran for the door.

* * * * *

Lorcan was livid. The desire to punish the man in front of him was almost overwhelming and the man knew it.

"Any idea how long he's been gone?" The barely controlled fury of his tone was unmistakable.

"No," Donal's voice quivered with fear. "He wasn't here when I got home an hour ago. As soon as I found him gone, I called Tomas. The security guard came on at five and he hadn't seen Kevin at all. The Secret Service didn't see him leave through the front, neither did their man on the service entrance. I have no idea how he got out."

Lorcan could smell the man's fear. He had to calm down. Donal could have done nothing about it. He wasn't even here when Kevin disappeared. Lorcan took a deep breath before speaking again. "Donal, I won't hurt you. I don't blame you. I don't know what he was thinking." His fists clenched in tight balls of rage. If Kevin left on a whim, when he found his wayward lover, they would have a serious heart-to-heart.

"Should we call the police?"

Lorcan could almost smell the fear and worry from the young man. The two men had become good friends. "The Secret Service knows he's missing?"

"Yes, I had to ask them." Donal's nervousness made the statement almost sound like a question.

"You did the right thing. Maybe their interference will be a benefit now. Have them come up. I want to speak with them."

Donal nodded then he left the room.

Tomas turned to Lorcan after the door closed. "You know he wouldn't let anything happen to Kevin. He's as upset as you are."

"I know, Tomas. I'm not angry with him. I'm angry with Kevin. I can't believe he would do this, but I can't think of how anyone could get past security. There's no sign of forced entry. Kevin wouldn't have opened the door to strangers." Lorcan fell into a nearby chair. "I promised I would keep him safe."

"If he left on his own, there was nothing you could have done."

Lorcan scrubbed his face with his hands. "I know. I wish we didn't have to live separately." His eyes stared at the door to Kevin's bedroom. His thoughts lingered on the last night in Kevin's bed, in his body. "If something happens to him, I will take revenge on Walter Chandler."

"I know."

Lorcan's throat tightened at the idea of losing Kevin. He closed his eyes against the pain. The two men sat without speaking, lost in their own private hell.

* * * * *

"Agent Malloy, come in." Anger over the Secret Service's interference turned to fury over their incompetence. "How the hell did he get past your men?"

"Mr. MacKenna," Malloy took a deep breath, "I want to offer my apologies for this. We only had one man on the service entrance. He didn't call for someone to replace him when he needed a break. He's been relieved of duty and will be reprimanded accordingly."

"Reprimanded?" Lorcan's fury made the man back up a step. "If something happens to Kevin, he'll have to worry about more than a reprimand!"

Lorcan turned away from Malloy before the desire to hurt him took complete control. He had to calm down. Killing the man wouldn't get Kevin back. As much as he despised Malloy, he needed his help. With a deep breath, he forced the anger down. "What have you done about Mr. St. James' disappearance?"

"We've contacted the local FBI and police. The FBI should be here within the hour. They'll want to set up a tap on the phones, both here and at your residence. If a kidnapper did this for money, they'll know you would be the source of possible payment."

"There won't be a ransom demand. This is Senator Chandler's doing."

The agent's mouth dropped in surprise. "What?"

"Mr. St. James has information that could be damaging to the senator's campaign. I know he threatened to reveal the information to the press if Chandler didn't back off and leave him alone. I have reason to believe Chandler was behind an attempt on Mr. St. James last winter."

"What does Mr. St. James know? And why haven't you mentioned it before now?"

"It's not my place to reveal it. Beside," Lorcan glared at Malloy, "why should we trust you? You work for the senator. I don't know why I should trust you now except I have no choice." Lorcan resisted the urge to pace.

"Mr. MacKenna, I don't work for the senator. I work for the government. There is a difference." Malloy frowned at the accusation. His eyes flared with the hint of anger but it was gone as quickly as it came.

"Then prove it."

"I need to know what accusations Mr. St. James has made against the senator."

"No. If Kevin wants to tell you, he will. When you find him."

Malloy's jaw twitched from his clenched teeth. "Fine. Does he have any evidence?"

Lorcan glowered at the man. If he said no, and the man was in league with the senator, Kevin was as good as dead. If he said yes, well, what proof could they have from a rape a dozen years ago? "No, it's Mr. St. James' word against the senator. I had him record the information in case something happened. It's safe where no one can find it."

"But it's something that can derail his bid for the presidency?"

"Yes, definitely."

Malloy looked thoughtful. His silence dragging out for several minutes.

Lorcan was about to speak.

The man nodded abruptly. "Okay. Don't say anything to the FBI about this. They might not be so understanding about Mr. St. James' privacy."

Lorcan nodded his agreement. Before he could say anything, a knock at the door interrupted them.

* * * * *

Lorcan sat in a corner of the room watching the FBI people set up their equipment. Donal was off to the side being questioned by yet another agent. The young man was holding up well to all the attention. His concern was very real for his friend and it showed as the concern for a lover. The clock read almost nine and Lorcan was getting antsy. He needed to do something rather than just wait. Unfortunately, he had no idea where to start.

He stood abruptly and stalked out of the room. He needed a little privacy. The feeling of helplessness was overwhelming. Why couldn't Kevin have stayed in the apartment? He knew why. His lover had been a virtual prisoner for the last eight months. His memory of being destitute would have faded. He was suffocating in his gilded prison. Lorcan had ignored Kevin's restlessness, thinking it was enough for them to be together once a week.

He punched the nearest wall and pain shot through his hand and arm, the drywall crumbling around his fist. He should never have agreed to Kevin moving out.

"He's not Mr. McCann's lover, is he?" Agent Malloy's voice was soft.

Surprised the man had managed to enter without Lorcan hearing him, even in his distracted state, Lorcan shook his head. "No, he's not." Lorcan didn't know why he should trust the man. But then, that day at Lorcan's apartment, the way Kevin stood up and took care of him, the fact had probably been obvious.

He didn't bother to turn around. "I'm a very private man, Agent Malloy. Kevin knew the scrutiny of the Secret Service would not be welcome. He insisted on this arrangement. I should have known better. Chandler needs to get rid of him. In spite of the attention, I should have kept him closer."

"We're doing everything we can to get him back. I don't work for Senator Chandler. If there's something he's done in the past that could be revealed in the campaign, I want to know what it is. My first duty is to the office of the president, not the man who holds the title. If the senator is unsuitable, I'd be the first to do something about it."

Lorcan turned to see the earnest expression in the agent's eyes. "Thank you."

"You're welcome."

"Can you do one thing for me?"

"Depends."

"Let the senator know there's a recording of Kevin's accusations. If Kevin's still alive, it might keep him that way."

The agent stared for a minute before giving Lorcan a quick nod. "Okay."

* * * * *

Lorcan wandered the streets until dawn, barely returning to his apartment before sunrise. He couldn't force himself to stay in the apartment not knowing where Kevin was. Not that wandering the streets did any good. Both Agent Malloy and the FBI agents objected but he insisted.

Lorcan sent Tomas back to the apartment with several men from the FBI to set up the taps on the phones there. If any calls came through, they could reach Lorcan by cell phone.

As the sunrise sapped his remaining strength, Lorcan slid into bed exhausted. He had to rest. Several days had passed since he fed. The anxiety and additional stress of wandering the streets for hours had taken its toll. If he didn't find Kevin, he would have to feed soon. He had no choice but to hunt prey on the street. No way he would use sex, not with his lover missing.

Tears formed and made slow tracks down the sides of his face as he stared at the ceiling. If Kevin were gone for good, he didn't know if he could go on. The loss of Gustave hadn't been this painful. He couldn't see a reason to continue without Kevin. The sorrow couldn't keep him from falling into an exhausted sleep. For once, he blessed his unnatural state. Vampires didn't dream. At least, he was safe from the nightmares that haunted him while awake.

* * * * *

Kevin was cold and his entire body hurt, his head most of all. His first thought was of Lorcan. His lover must have drunk too much. The weakness and lightheadedness were similar to the day after Lorcan first made love to him, first drank from him. The hard floor he lay on and the lack of warm blankets were the first clues to his situation.

His memory came flooding back. Donal. The hospital called. The cab he took had a familiar face driving it. The man from the alley, the one with the tattoo, who hit him, had grinned from the driver's seat as two other men climbed in the backseat surrounding him.

The memory of the man's cock in his mouth made Kevin gag.

"Sounds like he's awake."

Branded into Kevin's brain, the voice was the same. Footsteps announced his approach, a hard kick in Kevin's side heralded his arrival.

"You awake, pretty boy?"

Moving made Kevin realize his wrists were handcuffed and his feet were bound with rope.

"You aren't going anywhere. There are a few questions you have to answer."

"I'm not telling you anything." Kevin was relieved his voice didn't betray the sheer terror threatening to engulf him. A sharp kick in his stomach caused him to gasp for air.

"Well, evidently your boyfriend thinks he has something on your stepfather. So we need to know what it is and where you've stashed it. Otherwise, we might have to visit your boyfriend. Both of them."

"Go to hell." Another kick rewarded his answer. Kevin wasn't worried about Lorcan or Donal. When they discovered he was missing, they would be on their guard.

"You'll get there first. But whether you go quick and painless or slow, well, it's up to you."

"Oh like that's supposed to make me cooperate."

This time, his tormentor bent over far enough to slap his face. "Hey, guys," the man called out to the other men in the room, "he should be better at cock-sucking since he's been practicing with his two fancy boyfriends. I doubt they'd keep him around if he wasn't trainable." The man grabbed Kevin's face, squeezing hard. "I bet you've had your lips around both their cocks on a regular basis. Hell, you've probably learned to take it up the ass too."

He released Kevin's face with a push, forcing his head to crack on the concrete floor. For a few seconds, Kevin's sight blurred with swirling lights.

"If you cooperate, maybe we won't test you on your lessons." The laughter of the other men joined his captor's.

Although terrified, Kevin tried not to let the fear show. He didn't know what Lorcan meant by proof. His lover must have made something up, something to keep Kevin alive long enough to find him. He couldn't provoke these men. They might decide the information wasn't worth it and kill him without the answers they sought.

They had nothing to lose. Kevin knew their faces.

As much as he hated Walter for ruling his life, he suddenly decided he didn't want to die. Even worse, this dilemma was his fault. Sneaking out the service entrance was stupid. He hadn't wanted to explain himself to the Secret Service. Obviously a trap and he fell for it. From the man's words, Kevin at least knew Donal was okay.

Looking up into the cruel eyes, Kevin shook his head. "What I have is enough to ruin my stepfather and you'll never get it. Tell him if something happens to me, he'll be an outcast in Washington. He'll never be president. He won't be able to stay a senator and he'll end up disgraced and possibly in jail. You tell him before you even think about harming me."

Kevin was relieved to see a frown of uncertainty on the man's face. Maybe Lorcan's ruse would work for a while. But would it be long enough?

* * * * *

Once again Lorcan wandered the streets of the city. Rising at sunset, he barely waited for the last rays to disappear before leaving the apartment. If he were to keep up this pace, he would have to feed. As much as he hated hunting, he decided to feed several times tonight. With a large infusion of blood, he would be able to stay awake during the day.

Lorcan's breath caught in his throat. If he'd known the problems applying for a passport would cause, he would have done things different. Being immortal meant he had to change identities every dozen years or so. Others of his kind had a similar need. Vampires couldn't live together but they were required at least to cooperate with each other for their secretive survival. Their network would have easily provided Kevin with a new identity and a passport.

Lorcan could kick himself for not doing it in the first place. How could he have known it would get so complicated? The possibility of a new identity was still available. He had to find Kevin first.

Unsure of where to start, Lorcan paused in the middle of the sidewalk, still crowded enough for him to become an obstacle to the flow of pedestrian traffic. Walking the streets in search of his lover wasn't helping. He needed leverage. He needed to talk to the senator.

First however, he needed to feed.

A man bumped into him hard. A hand fumbled for his wallet.

Lorcan's lips curled into a small smile and his fangs began to extend. The man didn't realize he'd tried to pick the wrong pocket.

* * * * *

Lorcan's arrival at Kevin's apartment didn't strike the FBI agents or Agent Malloy as strange. Naturally, Tomas and Donal were a bit startled. It was ten in the morning and the day was hot in spite of the overcast skies. Personally, Lorcan was relieved the sky was cloudy. He hadn't ventured out during the day in nearly fifty years and he found it more daunting than he remembered.

To Lorcan's relief, Tomas and Donal controlled their expressions quite well. "Agent Malloy, may I speak with you in private?"

"Yes, sir," Malloy responded quickly.

Lorcan led him to the study, closing the door behind him.

Might as well come straight to the point. "I need to speak to the senator."

"Sir, there's still no evidence the senator is behind Mr. St. James' disappearance."

"I don't need evidence. He threatened Kevin shortly after he moved in here. The call was from a prepaid cell phone, untraceable. I will expose him if anything happens to Kevin. I want him to know that. You can't threaten a political figure. I can." Lorcan clenched his fists. He wanted to do more to Chandler than threaten him. "Tell me how to contact him. Without the red tape. I'm sure you know how. I want the number."

Malloy looked thoughtful for a moment. "I want to know what you have on the senator. I won't grant you access unless you tell me."

"You have your own suspicions, don't you?"

"I do. I can't tell you what they are. However, you can tell me what you know."

Lorcan thought about it for several seconds before he nodded. He had no choice but to trust this man. If Malloy was honest, he could help. If he wasn't, then he wouldn't live long after Lorcan discovered his duplicity.

"Sit." Lorcan motioned to a chair as he sat in the one opposite. "Chandler beat Kevin almost from the beginning. He was abusive to his wife as well. Possibly still is."

"Not enough to ruin him."

"No. But when Kevin was fifteen, Chandler raped him." Lorcan watched the agent's expression for his reaction. The shock was genuine or the man had a career in acting ahead. "That *would* ruin the good senator." Sarcasm dripped from Lorcan's lips like blood.

"It would."

"Does it fit with the information you have?"

"Actually, it does." Malloy looked a little startled at his own words. "I'll deny I ever said it."

"Said what?" Lorcan said with conspiratorial grin.

* * * * *

"Hello." The voice on the other end of the phone was deep, gruff-sounding.

"Senator Chandler?" Lorcan held back his rage at the man on the other end of the line. He had to stay calm for this conversation.

"Yes. Who is this?"

"A friend of Kevin's."

"How did you get this number?"

"I have connections." Lorcan smirked as he repeated the words Kevin said Chandler had used.

"What do you want?"

"I want you to know if anything happens to Kevin, I'll make sure your dirty little secret is plastered all over the media. No voter would want you in the White House after that. You won't keep your senate seat either."

"You have nothing on me. I'm not falling for blackmail."

"I don't know. Having a child rapist in the White House doesn't sound like something the American people would go for."

The sputtering on the other end of the phone was gratifying to Lorcan. He didn't give the senator time to regain his composure. "I would imagine the investigation following such allegations would bring out all kinds of information. Do you really want to spend your golden years in prison?"

Lorcan was guessing but Malloy's deliberate slip of the tongue made him think Kevin's rape wasn't the first or possibly the last. Pedophiles rarely had such control. Malloy must have found at least hints of another impropriety in Chandler's background. Lorcan wasn't above using it to get his lover home safe. "I'll make a deal with you. Give me Kevin and we'll disappear. You'll never hear from us again. Your dirty little secrets will be yours to deal with."

"I don't know where Kevin is. I had nothing to do with his disappearance." The quiver in Chandler's voice betrayed him. He knew and he was responsible.

Lorcan let the anger seep out and color his words. "Trust me. If anything happens to Kevin, you will regret it. For as long as you live." Lorcan's voice dipped to a growl. "Which, by the way, won't be long." Lorcan took a deep breath as he hung up the phone. Turning slowly, he looked at Malloy.

"You shouldn't have threatened him." Malloy shut off the recording device. "It won't look good."

"I don't care what it looks like. If a threat gets Kevin back, then I'll threaten him."

"You could end up in trouble if something happened to the senator."

"If something happens to Kevin, it won't matter. Besides, I am a very rich man. You'd never trace anything back to me." Vampires might be territorial and unwilling to live near each other but their complicated network of communication and cooperation helped them to survive in an ever-shrinking world. Lorcan only needed to send a message to the one who stalked the nation's capital. Chandler would be dead by dawn. Not even the Secret Service could protect him.

"I understand your feelings about Mr. St. James but I wish you hadn't said it on tape." Malloy's eyes were sympathetic but concerned.

Lorcan knew his action was foolish but he couldn't help himself. But Lorcan didn't make idle threats. Something about Malloy's expression made him think the man knew it.

Chapter Twelve

So far, his captors left Kevin alone. He didn't know how much time had passed since his kidnapping. His watch was gone and the room had no windows to indicate the hour. Handcuffs secured by a chain to a radiator meant freeing himself was impossible. They untied his feet when they let him go to the bathroom and left them loose. Chained to a radiator, he wasn't likely to go anywhere. His captors hadn't made good on their threats either. Kevin wasn't sure why but he was grateful for small favors.

All but one of the men had left. The one who remained, with the scarred face, was reading a paper but sat too far away for Kevin to see what the date was.

Between hunger and exhaustion, Kevin was sure he had been here at least a full day but didn't know how long he had been unconscious. His head still hurt but the blinding pain had given way to a dull, consistent throb. His wrists were raw from the handcuffs. At least, they cuffed his hands in front of him.

On his last trip to the bathroom, he managed to look around a little. The bathroom window had wood nailed over it. He wondered if he could pry the wood loose without his captors noticing. It would give him some idea of where he was or the time.

Speaking of... "Hey."

The man looked over the top of his paper with a bored expression. "What?"

"I need to use the bathroom."

"Humph." The paper covered his face again as he returned to his reading.

"Come on. I got to go!" Kevin's humiliation would be complete if he ended up wetting himself. Of course, it would be one more thing to amuse his tormentors. "Please!"

The paper rattled shut before the man tossed it on the table. He didn't bother to speak as he walked toward Kevin. He loomed over him for a moment before he grabbed the handcuffs around Kevin's wrists and undid the chain.

When the man yanked him to his feet and pushed him toward the door, the pain in his raw wrists nearly made Kevin lose his bladder control. Kevin closed the door, leaning against it until the painful throb of his wrists settled and the dizziness calmed.

The newspaper rattled in the other room. Maybe Scarface would stay engrossed in his paper for a while. Kevin took care of business as fast as he could then turned on the water in the sink. Splashing his face with cold water helped to calm his nerves. He needed to appear calm and invulnerable until Lorcan found him.

Leaving the water running, Kevin gently pried at one of the strips of wood over the window. He couldn't afford to make any noise. With no lock on the bathroom door, any suspicious sounds would bring his captor. The wood gave a slight bit. The elation at the tiny success was irrational but he gained a small illusion of control.

"What are you doing in there?" The voice was distant as if the man was still sitting at the table.

Kevin moved back to the sink, splashing water. "I'm just cleaning up." He dunked his head under the water to make his excuse seem more plausible.

"Well, get out of there." The chair legs scraped against the floor and the paper rattled again.

Grabbing some paper towels to dry off with, Kevin opened the door.

The man was still a few feet from the door when he came out. He followed Kevin to his corner and redid the chain before heading back to the table.

Kevin had to wait for another chance at the window. With any luck, he was on a low floor. Maybe he could escape on his own.

* * * * *

The heavy curtains pulled back, Lorcan watched the sunset from Kevin's room. The view of the city was magnificent. He hadn't seen a sunset in fifty years and it had been in London. The skyline of New York looked so different bathed in the dying sunlight. The night only revealed so much. Kevin was out there somewhere. Lorcan refused to believe he was dead. He was convinced he would feel the permanent loss of his lover. Somehow he would know when Kevin died.

The television droned on in the background. Senator Chandler and his wife had come to town. Chandler was playing up the grieving father, pleading for anyone to come forward with information about his missing son.

Lorcan sickened with disgust at the sound of the man's voice.

The silencing of the noise preceded Tomas' quiet words. "You need to rest."

"I can't."

"What you can't do is stay up forever. It won't help him for you to harm yourself."

"I know. And I'm...taking precautions."

"It's dangerous." Tomas knew exactly what precautions Lorcan required to maintain this pace.

Feeding several times a night, a lot of blood would spill until he found Kevin. The pickpocket was only the first of three last night. Lorcan had taken his rage out on the unfortunate man, leaving him to die in an alley. If someone found him quickly, he might have survived. A blush of shame heated Lorcan's face. He hadn't killed in so long. He hadn't meant to kill last night but the anger boiling below the surface had gotten the better of him. "I know."

Without further argument, Tomas' soft footsteps retreated.

A small victory in a sea of failures. He promised Kevin he would keep him safe. He failed. It didn't matter Kevin's own actions brought them to this point. Lorcan should have realized his lover was feeling caged. With a new identity, they could have traveled to Canada and then flown to Europe from there. Through the network of vampires, they could have easily lost anyone trailing them.

The familiar nightscape of New York now appeared. The strength supplied by the darkness returned. Time to hunt...for his lover and his next meal.

* * * * *

Kevin heard voices in the next room. Rather, one voice arguing with someone he couldn't hear. A telephone conversation? He strained to hear the words. The voice finally became recognizable, the tattooed cab driver, upset and angry.

"He's seen us! He knows who we are!"

A silent pause gave Kevin time to consider the words. A small tendril of hope wormed its way into Kevin. If the cab driver was worried about Kevin identifying them, whoever he was talking to might be telling him to let him go.

"I don't care what he can do to you! He can send us to prison!"

Hope blossomed slightly. Kevin was sure he understood the conversation. Now if only his captors obeyed their master.

"Well, then you'll have to forget your plans. I'm not going to prison over this."

Kevin's hope wilted.

"Okay, you have twenty-four hours. After that, we do things my way."

Twenty-four hours. His execution was scheduled. He had to get out of here. When the door opened, Kevin kept his eyes closed, hoping the man wouldn't realize he'd overheard the one-sided conversation.

*****

When the cell phone in his breast pocket vibrated, Lorcan was following his prey. The annoying noise angered him at first. With instinct in control, focused so completely on the hunt, it took Lorcan several seconds to remember the reason he was here.

Turning, Lorcan headed in the opposite direction of the thug he'd been following as he pulled the phone out of his pocket. A quick glance at the number told him it wasn't Tomas or Donal. He didn't recognize it.

"MacKenna," he barked into the phone.

"I have a deal for you."

Lorcan was surprised and then again, not surprised to hear Walter Chandler's voice on the other end. "What kind of deal?"

"I tell you where Kevin is and you...dispose of the men holding him."

"They're becoming more of a liability than Kevin?"

"You could say that. You have to come alone. I can't have the Secret Service involved or the FBI."

"Why?" Lorcan smelled a trap but he didn't care.

"You get Kevin out of the country and leave me alone. That was the deal."

Trap or no trap, Chandler couldn't know Lorcan was more than able to take out his henchmen. Lorcan's only concern was Kevin. If one of them got to Kevin before he could finish them off... "I'm listening." A part of him was glad he hadn't yet fed tonight. Nothing was more vicious than a pissed-off, hungry vampire.

*****

Lorcan watched the FBI men as they lounged around Kevin's apartment. Their apparent indifference to Kevin's disappearance made the rage seething below the surface hotter. Motioning for Tomas to follow him, Lorcan walked toward the study.

"Chandler's made a deal with me. He'll be calling back with instructions to meet the men who have Kevin." Lorcan kept his voice low.

"We should tell the FBI."

"Not part of the deal. I will handle it—alone."

"It's a setup."

"I know. Neither Chandler nor his men will be expecting what I have in store for them. We'll need to leave New York by morning. He's calling back in an hour. Once I have Kevin, I want to leave immediately."

"What if you fail?" Tomas' concern was valid.

"I won't. I can't."

Tomas gave him a hesitant nod. "What about Malloy? You seem to trust him."

"Only so far. He seems honest enough but I don't plan to leave any witnesses. I don't think he'd be a willing party to it."

Tomas sighed softly. "I'll make the arrangements, call the house in Canada, see if it's available and have them notify Serena you are coming. We should get new passports within a few days."

Vampires in transit commonly used the house Tomas mentioned. Serena was the resident vampire in Quebec. They had to notify her they would be in her territory, otherwise she would think someone was trespassing. A certain level of cooperation was afforded fellow vampires when they moved. Sooner or later, they all had to do it. Better to cooperate briefly than to fight. When she moved from New Orleans several years ago, Serena stayed a few days in New York.

Lorcan nodded as Tomas turned to leave the room. Now he had to wait for the phone call.

* * * * *

Kevin knew something was up. Three of the men were here. They had been taking turns at watching him since he first woke up. Only a few hours passed since the phone conversation sealed his fate so he hoped it wasn't a bad sign. Of course, if they knew he would die soon, they might have decided to test his "skills" before they killed him.

Each time Kevin went to the bathroom, he worked on loosening the boards over the window. With two nearly pulled free, he could see he was in a basement. If he could remove the boards, if he could get it open… The window didn't look as if it had a latch or was designed to open. The noise of breaking the glass would bring them into the bathroom too quick. There had to be a way to block the door for a minute or two.

Sitting quietly in the corner, he let a part of his mind work on the problem while another strained to hear their whispered conversation. His ears only caught snippets of sentences but he began to think they were expecting someone. His stepfather wouldn't get anywhere near this place or these men so it had to be Lorcan. Either his lover was close to discovering his whereabouts or they were planning an ambush. He needed to know more but he didn't want to draw their attention.

A cell phone interrupted their conversation.

"Yeah." The cab driver answered it. "I understand." He glanced at his watch. "Okay. We'll be ready." He snapped the phone shut as he turned toward Kevin.

"Well, we have a couple of hours to kill before we get to finish him and his boyfriend."

Walter must have found a way to lure his lover into a trap. He couldn't believe Lorcan would fall for it. If anything happened to Lorcan, Kevin would be to blame. By ignoring all the precautions Lorcan had taken to ensure his safety, he brought this on himself. His own death he could handle but Lorcan's... The soft moan had nothing to do with the three men surrounding him.

* * * * *

With his gift of stealth, Lorcan approached the warehouse. The sounds of the city faded as he concentrated on the building in front of him. Two cars were parked near a door in the middle of the building. At least two drivers, at least two people other than Kevin. He filed the information in the back of his mind.

A hint of light shone through a basement window. Cautious, his senses tuned into the slightest sound or movement, he approached it. Strips of wood across the window obscured most of his view but he could see through a slight opening. A bathroom, the door open, revealed a table covered in newspapers and paper cups. A way in, not the best way, but possible.

Moving slowly in the shadows, Lorcan drew near the cars. A slight noise, one so soft a human ear might not have caught it, stopped him in his tracks. One of the cars had an occupant. Standing in the shadows, he waited. Whoever watched must have changed position and settled back down.

Swift and silent, Lorcan moved to the car then yanked the door open.

The man inside scrambled for the gun sitting on the seat beside him but to no avail. His throat closed in Lorcan's tight grip right before inch-long fangs sunk into his jugular vein. He didn't even have time to scream.

* * * * *

The three men formed a half circle around Kevin's corner of the room. A couple of them were already rubbing their cocks through their clothes in anticipation. The cab driver had his pants open, ready for their fun and games.

Kevin was determined to put up a fight. What difference would it make? They would kill him anyway. Better to die before they raped him, rather than after.

"So let's see how good your mouth is now. Last time you weren't worth shit." The cab driver fisted his half-hard cock. "This time, I'll get my money's worth."

"Well, since you aren't paying me, it won't be much now, will it?" Kevin expected the blow for his sarcastic remark, but the sharp sting across his face still made him gasp.

"Your smart mouth will be much better occupied with my cock in it." He grabbed Kevin by the hair and pulled him up.

Pain shot through his neck as he found his face pressed against the man's groin. His mouth stayed shut. The roots of his hair were giving way under the intense pressure.

"You'll suck it or I'll be the first one up your ass. Your choice."

Kevin refused to speak for fear the man would take advantage of his open mouth. Instead, he tilted his head up, in spite of the pain, and glared at his attacker. Kevin saw the nod of his head to the other men. They moved in and grabbed him. He fought with all the strength he could muster. Weak from injuries and lack of food, it wasn't much but he at least hampered their efforts to undress him. A sharp blow to his head made him yell. Dizziness overwhelmed his movements. His last thought was at least he wouldn't be awake for what they did. Then the darkness swallowed him.

* * * * *

The half-moaned yell from inside had to be Kevin. Lorcan checked the door carefully. Locked and made of steel, he couldn't break it. Even with the fresh blood flowing through him, there were some limits to his strength. He ran back to the window. Peeking through the crack, the table, cleared of the newspapers and cups, now held Lorcan's lover, half nude and draped over the table facedown. Three men surrounded him, their cocks hard and ready as they pulled at the remaining clothes.

Grabbing a nearby trash can, Lorcan threw it with all his strength against the window. Glass shattered and wood splintered. The three men scrambled, leaving Kevin motionless on the table. Lorcan prayed he was only unconscious as he dove through the now-open window.

One man rounded the corner of the doorframe with a gun. Lorcan grabbed his throat and yanked. The satisfying sound of his larynx crushing sent a predatory glee through Lorcan's body. His fangs bared, he lunged through the door, diving to avoid the gunfire he was sure would follow.

His instincts paid off as the bullets fired above him, close enough to feel the hot metal whistling past. Rolling to his feet, he flew at a second man. In Lorcan's world, his victims moved in slow motion. His fangs bared with an animal growl, he went straight for the throat. His victim stared in shock, unable to move fast enough before Lorcan ripped his throat open. Blood flowed freely as the man fell to the floor, dead weight.

The blood of the second man running down his face, Lorcan moved toward the last one. This one he recognized as the man in the alley, the one who hurt Kevin. His death wouldn't be so easy.

"I'll kill him!" The man pointed his gun at Kevin. "I'll kill him unless you let me leave."

Lorcan stopped, gauging the man's stand, the way he held the gun, the shaking hand and the terror in his trembling voice. Could Lorcan take him before he pulled the trigger? This was the man who had been terrorizing Kevin. Could he let him walk away?

The sound of the gun firing rewarded his hesitation. The man didn't get another chance. His blood streamed down Lorcan's face before the gun clattered to the ground.

* * * * *

Kevin gasped at the intense pain in his back and stomach. In spite of the burning ache, he fought the arms pulling at him, turning him over. He wasn't going down without a fight. Slowly, his brain registered the sound of his lover's voice. "Lorcan?" His voice was weak to his own ears, distant.

Lorcan's voice seemed even farther away as strong arms tightened around him.

"Lorcan. I'm so sorry. I shouldn't have." Sharp pain stopped his words with a groan.

"Shhh… It's okay. Hang on. I've got to get you help."

Lorcan's hand pressed against his back, causing Kevin even more pain. "Oh God, what's wrong with me?"

"It's okay. I have to get you to a hospital. You'll be okay."

Lorcan's frantic words faded a little more. He wanted to tell Lorcan something, he needed to tell him. "I love you…" Kevin loved Lorcan.

His lover's voice sounded far away as he repeated his words. Lorcan still loved him in spite of what he had done.

Kevin heard what he needed to know then the world went black.

Epilogue

ഇ

"Lorcan?" Tomas' voice was soft as he entered the darkened room. "We'll be ready to leave in a few hours."

"Thank you." Lorcan stared at the night sky. The city of Quebec hadn't changed much in the ten years since he'd last been here.

Surprisingly, the deaths of the men at the warehouse hadn't hit the New York news yet, even after three days. Possibly the warehouse was as abandoned as it looked. Finding the bloody scene might take a while. Once the authorities identified Kevin's blood, there would be repercussions over the missing body.

Lorcan wasn't sure who the senator set up. The men in the warehouse had obviously been unaware of his approach since he'd caught them with their pants down, literally. They hadn't had time to hurt Kevin but they were all there, as if they were expecting trouble later. Maybe the senator hoped they would all kill each other and his secrets would be safe. Lorcan didn't know. It didn't matter anymore.

Malloy hadn't questioned Lorcan's abrupt departure but the FBI would have noticed it. If they put Kevin's blood together with the deaths of those men, Lorcan would be the prime suspect. Of course, the authorities hadn't yet found the fifth body.

The outcry over Senator Chandler's disappearance had been loud, receiving airtime on all the American as well as Canadian stations. It probably was headline news in England as well. The killer did a poor job of hiding the body so it wouldn't be much longer. An amateurish kill made out of the desire for revenge, Lorcan knew he should have been more careful but time hadn't permitted.

"Lorcan?"

A rush of bittersweet joy filled him as Lorcan turned toward his lover. "Come here." He held his arms out to Kevin.

"You look so sad," Kevin whispered as he moved into Lorcan's embrace.

"It's... I love you so much. You know that, don't you?"

"Yes. I'm sorry I've caused all this trouble. I shouldn't have left the apartment. I should have realized the phone call was a setup."

"It's done. We can't change it now. You're safe. And I plan to keep you that way for as long as I can."

Kevin raised his head to look at Lorcan. "Make love to me?"

As usual, what Kevin wanted, Kevin got. Lorcan's lips melted onto his. The kiss was gentle, full of feeling and emotion. Lorcan pulled Kevin toward the bed, enjoying the slow journey with their mouths locked. Hardening arousal bumped against Lorcan's erection as they moved. A small groan escaped his lips as they fell onto the bed. Kevin's weight was heavy, grounding him. He wanted this to last forever. The kiss grew hungrier, deeper, and a slight sob mixed in with their tangled tongues. Lorcan wasn't sure if the sound was his or Kevin's. Maybe both.

Lorcan rolled them until he was on top. He kissed his way down Kevin's chin to his throat. His fangs itched as he kissed his way down the glorious neck. Hands furiously tore at buttons until Kevin's chest was bare. Lorcan's mouth wanted to be everywhere at once but settled on the tiny tight flesh of his right nipple.

Kevin gasped as he suckled the sensitive nub.

Lorcan's hand moved down to find the hard flesh hidden by his jeans. Lorcan wanted him, wanted everything he could get as long as he could. Lorcan needed this, needed to feel his lover's heat and hardness, Kevin's lean body against his.

Standing, Lorcan pulled at his own clothes, shedding them as Kevin stripped his jeans. Lorcan's mouth zeroed in on his lover's cock, licking the tip, running his tongue down the hot shaft to the base. A strong hand pulled at his leg until his thighs straddled his lover's head. Kevin's mouth was molten heat around Lorcan's aroused flesh. He moaned against Kevin thigh as his hips automatically thrust into his lover's willing mouth.

Kevin took it, his hands pulling his hips, urging his motion.

Lorcan eagerly sucked his lover deep as his own arousal increased. He wouldn't last long and he wanted more from this encounter.

"Stop, Kevin. Please…" He pulled away from the hot, moist cavern before he rolled off Kevin. "I want to be inside you."

"Yes. Oh God, yes." Kevin's hand fumbled for the lube they stashed under the pillow.

Lorcan nearly came when a lube-filled hand stroked his cock.

Kevin moved over him, straddling his hips, his hand feeling for Lorcan's cock to guide it into him. With exquisite slowness, Kevin pushed down on the hard flesh, his body accepting the invasion with a groan of pleasure. An eternity passed before his lover's body fully engulfed him.

A slow rocking motion began as Lorcan's hands moved up Kevin's body. The soft skin covering hard muscles, the tiny nipples hard with desire, it was the most beautiful sight Lorcan had ever seen. His eyes filled with tears at the thought of losing this, losing him.

Kevin bent over to kiss his eyes, his nose, his lips. They locked mouths in a fierce battle of tongues. Devouring each other's moans, Kevin moved faster as Lorcan's hips thrust up to meet him.

The leaking hardness of Kevin's cock rubbed against his stomach. A harsh moan came from his lover as hot seed spurted onto Lorcan's stomach. As the tight ass clenched around him, Lorcan joined him.

Kevin arched up, his body jerking as Lorcan's seed filled his lover. A moan of pleasure escaped Kevin's open mouth. Lorcan looked up to see the bliss on his face.

His own joy diminished as, half extended in Kevin's mouth, he spotted glistening fangs.

Lorcan had known it couldn't last forever but he had hoped for more than barely a year. Soon Kevin's new desires would drive him from Lorcan's side, Lorcan's bed. Until then, he would try not to question the decision made in desperation, try not to mourn the loss of a lover who yet lived but couldn't stay with him. Tonight, they found satisfaction in each other's bodies but eventually...

Kevin collapsed on Lorcan. His sweat added to the slickness of his spilled seed. With breath still ragged from passion, Kevin gasped, "I know what you're thinking." He raised his head enough to meet Lorcan's gaze. "And it won't happen. We'll find a way to stay together, a way to make it work."

Gentle lips grazed his and their breath mingled. His throat tight with emotion, he simply nodded. Could this time be different? Could they, together, find a different path? Why not? For a life with Kevin, he'd battle demons at the gates of hell.

Losing himself in his lover's kiss, Lorcan let hope blossom and determination grow. Suddenly, the curse of endless darkness stretched into a promise of eternity.

Enjoy an excerpt from:
BURNING HUNGER

Copyright © TAWNY TAYLOR, 2007.
All Rights Reserved, Ellora's Cave Publishing, Inc.

∽

Hot, sweet blood streamed down Marek's throat, sending pulsing waves of raw energy through his tired body and urgent need to his groin. He jerked the woman closer, eager to take his fill of both her blood and her body. Yet no matter how firmly her softening form molded to his, and no matter how eagerly he drank, he could not get his fill of either.

More!

He drew in another mouthful of her blood. The unfamiliar sound of his heartbeat, slow and wavering but growing steadier, thumped in his ears. Strength returned to his arms and legs. The overwhelming weariness that had nearly overtaken him slowly lifted.

More!

He pulled in a third mouthful of energizing blood. She whimpered, lifted her arms and draped them over his shoulders. Her legs straddled one of his and her hips ground into his thigh as his heat burned into her.

"Ohhh…" she said on a sigh.

More, more, more!

Dayne's growl of protest stopped him from taking what his body demanded. He would kill her if he didn't stop now. They had seven nights to get their fill. Although he craved complete and immediate satisfaction, he knew receiving it would come at a great price. To all three of them.

Meeting Dayne's gaze, Marek gently pushed the flushed, dazed woman toward him, encouraging Dayne to take what he needed. She cried out, visibly disappointed by his apparent rejection. But when Dayne eased her around, swept her hair aside and sank his fangs into her porcelain skin, her expression turned wanton once more.

Agonizing lust simmered in his veins as he watched his new blood-mate drink. The expression in Dayne's eyes turned fierce, erotic, as he pulled in a second mouthful of the woman's blood, stirring Marek's lust to even more painful heights.

Driven by his need, he ripped the back of the woman's shirt down the center, revealing a stripe of silky skin marred by an ugly black strap.

He groaned.

The woman whispered, "Oh yessss…"

He unfastened her bra and gently lowered her arms, pressing his length against her back. His hips rocked as he removed her clothing from her upper body, driven by a different kind of hunger surging through his system. A sexual hunger.

Dayne lifted his head, releasing her neck. The bloodstained mark on her skin vanished instantly. His tongue swept over his lips, an invitation.

It was done. Dayne was now bound to him, and he to Dayne. For the first time in his life, he was overcome by sexual hunger for another man.

Driven by instinct, Marek hooked a hand behind Dayne's head and with the woman's writhing body between them, claimed his mouth. Their tongues battled, stabbing, stroking while the woman's soft derriere pillowed his cock and balls, the scent of fresh spring air and delicate flowers teased his nostrils and her feminine whimpers and sighs filled his ears.

The agony and ecstasy.

Senses that had slowly faded over the centuries were suddenly painfully sharp, a contrast so severe it nearly drove him mad. He could hear the gusting of air as she exhaled. Could smell the musk of her need. Could feel the cool silk of Dayne's hair twining around his fingers.

He broke the kiss, instead turning his attention to the woman who'd given him so much. By the simple act of being there, submitting to their needs, she'd given both of them a chance at another five hundred years of life. She would get her reward.

The clue she wanted. The dominant lovers she craved. And the release she demanded.

* * * * *

Oh my God! They're kissing each other? They're bi? That is so hot.

Brea's body was burning up. She was the meat in a Chippendale sandwich and God help her, she was loving it! Smooshed between two hot, impossibly sexy bodies, her shirt gone, her bared nipples teased to aching erection by the delicious friction against Number One's shirt. Two sets of hands were exploring each other then her body, easing her out of the rest of her clothes, smoothing up her arms and down her sides. Two mouths were tickling her neck and shoulders with teasing kisses and soft nips.

Two voices murmured seductive promises.

Who would have thought it was possible? To be so lost? To experience such overwhelming need?

Before she fully realized it, she was unclothed and so were they.

Two perfect bodies. Toned, tanned and both possessing a latent power that stole the oxygen from her lungs.

Their expressions mirrored each other's, both dark with desire. It was their looks, the heat she saw simmering in their eyes that drove her backward, until the back of her legs struck what she quickly realized was the bed.

That was one enormous adult playground.

Number One caught her hands in his fist and lifted her arms over her head. He stepped closer until his huge frame completely invaded her personal space, both driving her crazy with desire and making her feel slightly uncomfortable at the same time.

It was a bizarrely thrilling combination—discomfort and desire.

"I can smell your arousal," he murmured, his eyes searing her skin as his gaze swept over her face. "The fear intensifies your reaction."

Did it ever!

Was that why she wasn't screaming for her life? Was that why she wasn't kicking him in the gonads or at least begging him to stop? She'd never had sex with a complete stranger, let alone two. She didn't even know their names.

God, how bad was that?

"You have been secretly yearning for this for a long time." He pulled slightly, forcing her hands higher in the air. Her biceps sandwiched her head, pressing against her ears and muffling sounds, his voice. Her racing heartbeat pounded in her head. "You want a man to take control in the bedroom."

She did. She really, really did.

No. This was so wrong! Control? Absolutely not. Sleeping with men she didn't know. Kidnappers. Bad men. They were bad.

But they looked soooooo good. And felt soooo amazing.

He gathered both of her wrists into one fist and twisted, forcing her to turn her body to the side, where Number Two was kneeling.

"Spread your legs," Number Two demanded.

No doubt what would happen next. A gush of heat pulsed to her core as she met his gaze. A split second later, a spike of guilt stabbed her insides. She was crazy if she did anything with these guys. A shameless hussy. She hadn't been raised like this—to fuck the first kidnapping Chippendale she stumbled upon...or first pair of kidnapping Chippendales.

Time to reclaim some of her scruples, to recover her brain out of the thick fog that had somehow enveloped it.

How had she gotten to this point anyway?

One minute she'd been talking about a job as a personal waitress...or something like that. And then what?

She looked down at her clothes, lying in a heap on the floor. How'd her shirt get ripped? Why couldn't she remember? Was there anything to remember? Of course there was.

Her neck tingled, burned like she'd scratched it. After Number One released her wrists, she pressed her fingertips to the sore spot, the chill easing the pain.

As she struggled to gather her thoughts, she lifted her chin, an intentional show of defiance. "No."

Number One's formerly charming smile turned wicked and a little threatening, utterly sexy. "But you've given us so much. Don't you wish to receive your reward?"

Why an electronic book?

We live in the Information Age—an exciting time in the history of human civilization, in which technology rules supreme and continues to progress in leaps and bounds every minute of every day. For a multitude of reasons, more and more avid literary fans are opting to purchase e-books instead of paper books. The question from those not yet initiated into the world of electronic reading is simply: *Why?*

1. *Price.* An electronic title at Ellora's Cave Publishing and Cerridwen Press runs anywhere from 40% to 75% less than the cover price of the exact same title in paperback format. Why? Basic mathematics and cost. It is less expensive to publish an e-book (no paper and printing, no warehousing and shipping) than it is to publish a paperback, so the savings are passed along to the consumer.

2. *Space.* Running out of room in your house for your books? That is one worry you will never have with electronic books. For a low one-time cost, you can purchase a handheld device specifically designed for e-reading. Many e-readers have large, convenient screens for viewing. Better yet, hundreds of titles can be stored within your new library—on a single microchip. There are a variety of e-readers from different manufacturers. You can also read e-books on your PC or laptop computer. (Please note that Ellora's Cave does not endorse any specific brands.

You can check our websites at www.ellorascave.com or www.cerridwenpress.com for information we make available to new consumers.)

3. ***Mobility.*** Because your new e-library consists of only a microchip within a small, easily transportable e-reader, your entire cache of books can be taken with you wherever you go.

4. ***Personal Viewing Preferences.*** Are the words you are currently reading too small? Too large? Too… ANNOYING? Paperback books cannot be modified according to personal preferences, but e-books can.

5. ***Instant Gratification.*** Is it the middle of the night and all the bookstores near you are closed? Are you tired of waiting days, sometimes weeks, for bookstores to ship the novels you bought? Ellora's Cave Publishing sells instantaneous downloads twenty-four hours a day, seven days a week, every day of the year. Our webstore is never closed. Our e-book delivery system is 100% automated, meaning your order is filled as soon as you pay for it.

Those are a few of the top reasons why electronic books are replacing paperbacks for many avid readers.

As always, Ellora's Cave and Cerridwen Press welcome your questions and comments. We invite you to email us at Comments@ellorascave.com or write to us directly at Ellora's Cave Publishing Inc., 1056 Home Avenue, Akron, OH 44310-3502.

Make each day more *EXCITING* with our

Ellora's Cavemen Calendar

www.EllorasCave.com

Cerridwen, the Celtic Goddess of wisdom, was the muse who brought inspiration to storytellers and those in the creative arts. Cerridwen Press encompasses the best and most innovative stories in all genres of today's fiction. Visit our site and discover the newest titles by talented authors who still get inspired - much like the ancient storytellers did, once upon a time.

Cerridwen Press
www.cerridwenpress.com

ELLORA'S CAVE
ROMANTICA PUBLISHING

Discover for yourself why readers can't get enough of the multiple award-winning publisher

Ellora's Cave.

Whether you prefer e-books or paperbacks,

be sure to visit EC on the web at
www.ellorascave.com

for an erotic reading experience that will leave you breathless.

Made in the USA